THE BONE TAKER

TAKER

(CREEPTOWN #2)

Scott Charles

First paperback edition April 2021

Paperback ISBN: 978-1-7361521-3-3
Digital ISBN: 978-1-7361521-2-6

Published by Yellow Morning Press

Illustration copyright © 2021 by Florian Garbay

1

WHEN MY FRIEND DARIUS found the missing *C. rex* skeleton that half the town was searching for, at first I didn't believe him.

No way could he find it. No way.

How could a twelve-year-old kid find a missing museum exhibit that not even my uncle Leo could find?

"The museum staff has been searching all afternoon for that," I told him. "I think Uncle Leo would've noticed a forty-foot skeleton reappearing."

Maybe, I thought privately.

"I'll prove it," Darius insisted. "Follow me."

He nodded to the very back of the museum hall. *One of the corridors.*

My heart shivered.

Where were we, exactly? Would you believe me if I said we were on a class trip to the Museum of Natural History? Not the real one in New York City. This was my uncle Leo's version.

Kind of.

The museum building was brand new, and there was a thrilling mystery attached to it. Basically, nobody knew who had built it, who had paid for it, or who in their right mind had looked around at all the job applications flooding in from Harvard and Stanford and Duke and said, "Ah! Yes! The D+ student from Cretaceia College, Class of 2002! *That's* the person I must put in charge!"

But all of it really happened.

Like Cinderella when she married the prince, Uncle Leo left his job scrubbing dishes at Wexley's and became Executive Director of the Museum of Natural History—this freaky, huge place, full of paintings and statues and long, bendy corridors that never seemed to lead to the room you expected, like in *Harry Potter* or something.

"Hogwarts," my teacher had called it. "On Friday morning, for our class trip, we'll be visiting the closest thing to a real Hogwarts castle."

Was it true? Was Ms. Wellington right?

In a minute, I'll let you judge for yourself.

"C'MON," DARIUS HISSED. "That corridor could disappear any second. We have to go *now*."

I puffed out a breath. My eyes slid to Mrs. Fawcett, our chaperone. Was she watching us?

No. Her famous death glare was fixed on a Greek statue in the corner. I think the naked body offended her.

Everything offends Mrs. Fawcett.

"Hurry, Arlo. Before the old bag turns around!"

"Okay, okay. Fine."

Darius and I pretended to walk toward the restrooms, then swerved down a corridor that seemed to grow bigger as soon as we entered it.

I took slow, careful steps instead of speed-walking.

Don't squish, I begged my ankles. *Don't wrinkle. Don't flop.*

Darius raced out ahead of me. I watched his bookbag straps whip round the bend, heading God knows where.

"Darius?" I called nervously. "Darius?"

I shuffled after him, squishing and flopping. My heart pounded. Did I mention how eerie these corridors were? Do you know about the slime dripping down? The space-black windows? The weird, bloody light?

How about my legs? The missing bones in my legs?

I let out a long, wheezy breath as I finally emerged out the other end of the corridor. I blinked my eyes, peering round. The new room was totally strange. No ceiling. No walls. Just a wide open space filled with fog.

Fog and bones.

About ten seconds later, I found the missing *C. rex* skeleton.

It opened its jaw bone and lunged at me.

2

THE CRAZIEST, SPOOKIEST, most bone-flopping day of my life started six hours earlier, with a dinosaur bone on my doorstep.

THWACK!

A sharp noise echoed over the porch, just as I slid down the staircase and into the kitchen. Dad looked up from his oatmeal. There was a second THWACK! as his *Fossil Fan* magazine dropped.

"How many times, Arlo?" he scolded. "No sliding down the banister!"

"But Dad," I said. *"My ankles."*

Dad's eyebrows scrunched up, like they always did when I mentioned my bone stuff. "Check the porch," he growled. "That sound should be one of your...*treatments* arriving."

I rolled my eyes.

My dad is a college professor. It's his job to know the answers to things. So he gets really cranky whenever he's stumped by a question. He hates that no one can explain my condition.

Last year, he drove me all the way to Arizona to visit the famous Mayo Clinic hospital. The doctors there took one look at my X-ray and screamed.

"B-Bones!" they cried. "Where are your *bones*, child?"

"How is he *alive*? How can he *stand it?*"

Would you believe me if said I *couldn't* stand it? Not then. Not for one second longer. My bones squished and I sank to the floor like a lump of spaghetti.

My name is Arlo Vreeland. I'm twelve, and everyone I meet asks the same exact question. If I'm really unlucky, they scream it.

"ARLO! WHERE ARE YOUR BONES?"

"You're asking me," I like to say, "but who am I supposed to ask?"

The truth is, I'm all right most of the time. I'm a nice, normal kid.

Just bendy.

With the right focus, I can walk normally. I even jog sometimes. Most people would never know that I'm missing up to forty percent of my bones.

The only trouble is when I get scared. If something startles me, if I lose concentration…well, that's when things can get messy.

Beneath my tan skin with all the fuzzy red hairs twisting out (more than anyone else in my grade) I have sixty to seventy percent of a full human skeleton.

Guess what else? I'm losing more all the time.

That's why I was pretty careful as I crossed the kitchen to our tiny front door.

Don't slip, I warned myself. *Don't squish and collapse.*

I gripped the handle and pulled. The door opened barely an inch. Oops. I was so busy focusing, I'd forgotten to unhook the latch.

Not that I needed to.

"Ugh, fine," I said, moving forward. My bones squished as I slid through the gap. A second later, I popped out the other side.

Really.

A cool breeze touched my face. I stepped into the sunlight, toward a ball of crumpled-up newspaper that sat on the porch. There was no label attached.

Not good, I thought. *Dad must really be panicking.*

Any company that shipped its products without a bag or a box was probably sketchy. But what choice did we have? I really, really needed my bones back. Maybe one of Dad's crazy treatments might actually work.

But probably not, I thought grimly.

Feeling helpless, I reached for the newspaper bundle.

"RaaaawWWWwwwwRRRrrr!!!"

There was a horrible roaring sound. Pain shot up my arm as a set of razor-sharp teeth bit my knuckles.

I screamed out in terror.

3

"FLUFFKINS!" CRIED A VOICE. "Fluffkins, no! Don't bite the stranger!"

A tall woman with a helmet of stiff yellow hair came scurrying onto the porch. She scooped up the scruffy brown dog that attacked me.

A chihuahua. A demon dog.

My skin slurped like molasses as Fluffkins' teeth slipped down my fingers.

"Hi, Carlo," said the woman. "Fluffkins didn't mean it. Did you, Fluffy-poo? Kisses! *Muah, muah, muah!*"

She kissed Fluffkins a gazillion more times, then skipped away without even apologizing.

Do I know her name? Yes.

Does she know my name? No.

Fair is fair. Why should I write her name in my book?

Eyes slitted, I grabbed the sopping-wet bundle and slithered into the house. What was in this thing? Dog food? A human heart?

I slammed the door angrily. There was a CLUNK! as a large object fell out of the wrapping and onto our *Dr. Fossil Says Welcome!* mat.

I stared down at it. "Whoa."

I was expecting to see a pile of shattered glass or a test tube that leaked on the floor. Some top secret product Dad had found on the Internet.

That wasn't it, though.

Not even close.

I was still staring when Dad finally took interest. He set his magazine down and walked over. Scooping the giant white bone off the floor, he sank into a trance as he closely examined it.

"Hmmm. *Archaeopteryx?* No, *Stegosaurus.* Late Jurassic. A shin bone, perhaps?"

He turned to me, blinking back to reality.

"Arlo Vreeland, where on God's green Earth did you *find* this?"

My face paled. I started patting my rib cage and flexing my knees. *Did I lose another bone? Was that my bone on the floor?*

My thoughts were a little insane. Before I could answer, Dad let out a roar. His face purpled and his bushy eyebrows got all scrunched together.

"Sacrilege! Vandalism! THAT SCOUNDREL!"

Dad's hands were shaking. He stared in horrified shock at the shin bone. I leaned closer. There were words etched on top of the bone.

To Arlo Vreeland — ADMIT ONE
You are cordially invited to THE MUSEUM OF NATURAL HISTORY, now featuring America's newest dinosaur, the *Creeposaurus rex!* Present this fossil at the gate for special Forbidden Zone access.

"T-T-This is a priceless artifact!" Dad stammered. "*The college* donated these bones. He's – he's supposed to protect them!"

"Can't you sandpaper the words off?" I asked.

I thought it was pretty funny.

"One hundred and fifty million years old," Dad grumbled. "And he's engraving them! He treats them like napkins!"

Dad was talking about Uncle Leo, of course. The museum director.

His brother.

Uncle Leo has what Mom calls "a checkered past." Growing up, he used to visit us every few months. It was fun for me. I love Uncle Leo. But on every visit, during dinner, I remember Dad would lean forward and say, "How much is it this time, Leo?" And Uncle Leo would tell me to go upstairs (but I wouldn't) then say something like, "The car broke down, Harry, I need a hundred dollars. This is the last time, I swear."

"My good-for-nothing brother," Dad called him.

That was before the Museum of Natural History job that changed Uncle Leo's life—and kind of ruined my dad's.

I told you, Dad is a college professor. His full title is "Dr. Harold Vreeland, The John H. Ostrom Chair of Paleontological Science at Cretaceia College," although the sign on his office door has a different name on it.

Yes. Dr. Fossil.

So you can imagine Dad's reaction when he found out his priceless fossils would be shipped to Uncle Leo's museum for safe-keeping. Uncle Leo is practically Dad's boss now.

How ironic is that?

DAD STILL WASN'T finished complaining.

"And — and that *Creeposaurus* nonsense!" he ranted. "What a joke! Any *trained* paleontologist will tell you that 'brand-new' skeleton of his—okay, yes, it's remarkably well-preserved for its size—but it isn't groundbreaking, either! It's a *Tyrannosaurus rex.* Just a *T. rex!* Not some kooky new species!"

Dad's chest was heaving. He was really worked up.

"The fool obviously put the bones in the wrong order. That explains the discrepancies. The strange dorsal vertebra. The so-called…*fangs.*"

"Fangs?" I said. "Poison fangs?"

Dad rolled his eyes. "This is why fossil work should be left to professionals, Arlo. Museums are glorified gift shops. A trained monkey could work one. By contrast, that same monkey would need an advanced degree and several years of dig site experience before teaching at Cretaceia College."

"*And* a minor in spelling," a voice added, giggling.

Mom sauntered into the room, fully dressed in her work clothes.

"Excited for your field trip, Arlo?" She picked the bone up and peered through her glasses. "Wow, *Creeposaurus rex!* How interesting!"

"It's not real," Dad grunted.

Mom's eyes lit up. "What if it is?" she said, nudging me.

Dad reached for his briefcase, ignoring her. "Arlo, my boy, I want you to be my eyes and ears in that museum today. You're a movie guy, right? Bring your camera. I want a close-up view of this so-called *Creeposaurus rex.*"

He passed me a packet full of squiggles and shapes.

"Bone diagrams," he explained. "When you're taking pictures, pay special attention to the ischium and tarsus regions. You know what they say: if the tarsus won't fit, you can *forget* the phalanges!"

He gave a honking laugh.

Paleontologists are seriously weird.

With a long sigh, I took the packet from Dad and slipped it into my pocket. Yes. My class trip had just turned into a homework assignment.

I was pretty annoyed. I didn't want anything to do with Dad and Uncle Leo's fight. Even if I did, I wouldn't necessarily take Dad's side.

I told you, I like Uncle Leo. He's goofy and strange, just like me. Plus he's a riot. People love him.

That's why, deep down, I hoped the *Creeposaurus rex* was real. I felt a thrill of excitement imagining a *T. rex* with

11

giant, hooked fangs. I couldn't wait to be in the same room with a forty-foot, man-eating skeleton.

Okay, *dino-eating*. The ultimate predator.

"RAAAWWWWRRRR!"

I let out a yelp as Dad's phone alarm suddenly howled. "Paging Dr. Fossil," it continued. "Dr. Fossil. Dr. Fossil."

"Time to go," said Dad, standing up. "I have a very important class to teach. Unlike *some people* in the family."

He gave a *"hmph!"* in the invisible direction of Uncle Leo, kissing Mom's ink-black hair on his way out the door.

When I looked up, I noticed Mom's eyes were twinkling again. "And which *important class* are we teaching today?" she asked Dad.

Blood drained from his face. He nibbled his lip.

"The, er, biology," he half-mumbled, "of dinosaurs."

"Oh, how *intriguing!*" Mom gasped. "Silly me, I thought paleontologists wouldn't know the first thing about dino biology. All we have are the bones. Isn't that right?"

"Well, ah…it's very complicated. Very important."

Dad slipped the latch and rushed out the door.

Would you believe it if I told you he screamed?

4

"AAAAAHHHHHH!" Dad shrieked.

"Oh hey, Dr. V!" Darius's deep voice rolled through the doorway. "Did my dinosaur scare you? Lifelike, isn't it? It's the *Creeposaurus rex!* Well, me and Arlo's version of it. We adapted it from the Cine-Blocks kit."

"Must—be—going," Dad gasped, rushing off.

I craned my neck out the doorway.

"'Sup Arlo!" Darius waved his Cine-Blocks dinosaur. "How's it going? Bones still together?"

"Barely," I muttered.

Darius Moreland is probably my best friend at the moment. He's a big, chubby kid with frizzy black hair and a bullfrog-type voice. I guess he's not the coolest guy in the universe. Then again, who am I?

Darius and I are both really big into Cine-Blocks. Cine-Blocks are like Legos, only way more realistic. I love the clicking sound of joining pieces together. Plus the things I make never flop or fall over.

With enough kits, you can make *anything* out of Cine-Blocks. Literally anything.

Guess what Darius makes?

"Yo, check it out! New Creeps for the trip!"

Darius reached into his blue Jansport bookbag (which has never once held a schoolbook) and pulled out four new creations.

All dinosaurs.

I noticed the fangs right away. "Dad would have a heart attack if he saw these," I chuckled.

Darius beamed. "Awesome, right? I adapted your *T. rex* kits for the movie! If we zoom in, they'll look like normal-sized Creeps. No one will know the difference!"

"What about live shots?" I asked. "Actors can't share the screen with Cine-Blocks. It looks totally fake."

"True," said Darius. "For those, we'll need human-sized monsters. *Bigger* than human-sized." His eyes glimmered. "We'll need...the *Creeposaurus rex* skeleton!"

He leaned back and gave a stunningly lifelike "RAAWWR!"

"Yeah, I've been practicing." He grinned at my shocked expression.

In case you haven't guessed, Darius and I were making a movie. We'd been planning it for weeks, ever since Darius came up with his genius idea.

Yes. We were going to film it *today*, at the Museum of Natural History. All those bendy corridors and spooky exhibits would become the background and props of our movie.

And how much would it cost us? Nothing. Zilch!

How genius was that?

Originally, I'd only agreed to build the Cine-Blocks props. But Darius can be really persistent (a.k.a. kind of annoying) and pretty soon I got roped into playing the lead role, Dr. Arlo Vreeland.

Darius was directing. I knew he wanted to get my boneless body on film as part of the climax. It was the main reason he cast me.

But not the *only* reason. (More on that later).

I flipped through the screenplay he e-mailed me.

"This is...a lot of scenes," I gulped. "Are you sure Ms. Wellington will be okay with us filming instead of joining the tour group?"

"Who cares?" said Darius. "School is for dorks."

"Some of us want to *pass* the sixth grade," I pointed out.

Darius grinned. "I'm an artist, Arlo. Making movies *is* my school." He hesitated. "Can I borrow your math homework when we get on the bus?"

I rolled my eyes at him.

NORMALLY, OUR WALK to the bus stop was short. Barely two driveways. You round the corner and poof— it's right there.

So how come we hadn't arrived yet?

Why were we passing our *seventeenth* driveway?

Darius raised our *Creeposaurus rex* models into the air, making roaring sounds as he skipped down the sidewalk.

"Not so loud," I hissed. "What's the point of avoiding Craig Stetler's house if you're going to scream our location?"

"Stetler would make a good villain," Darius mused. "I wonder if he knows how to act?"

"He knows how to strangle," I muttered.

Darius's roaring grew louder. He started spinning around, doing loop-de-loops with the Creeps.

"Slow down!" I hissed. "I can't keep up with you!"

My kneecaps were shaking. Since I was about to flop over, I took my eyes off the street for one second.

One second.

And within that one second, Darius crossed the last driveway before the bus stop, hopped the curb, and skipped straight into oncoming traffic!

Okay, not a car or a bus.

Something worse.

THUMMMMP! CRAAACK!

"BOOOOMMMM!" roared a voice. "Stetler Smash!"

A second later, the *Creeposaurus rex* models that we had carefully built over six or seven hours went SPLAT! on the pavement.

I stared in shock at the skittering pieces.

Stetler. Craig Stetler.

He'd found me!

5

CRAIG STETLER IS BAD NEWS. He's just a really rough kid, unfortunately. Stetler is almost six feet tall. He has a mean face, bulging muscles and (least importantly) no hair at all. Not even eyebrows.

On another planet, in some alternate, Earthlike dimension, Stetler and I might've been friends. Ask me if I know what it's like to be strange.

Because I do. I absolutely do.

But that doesn't mean I go around roughing people up. I don't pick fights after school. I don't specifically target the other strange people (like me) who weren't born with big, bulging, Hercules muscles.

"Whatcha looking at, freak?" Stetler's thin, shark-like eyes locked onto me. "This is my bus stop. Why should I let a boneless freak ride my bus?"

"I have to get to school," I mumbled.

My heart was pounding. I couldn't stop staring at my broken Cine-Blocks. Why, *why* did Darius have to rush to the bus stop? Why couldn't he wait until the bus arrived, like I asked him to?

"Speak up, freak. I can't hear your little freak voice."

I swallowed. "I have to get to school. *Please.*"

"Then you need to pay the toll." Stetler leered at me. "Today's toll is three dollars. Wait, no it isn't. It's ten."

"Ten dollars!?"

My gift shop money.

I bit my lip. I was trying to think. Trying to—

"Owww!" I uttered a cry as Stetler punched my left arm. The skin started crazily rippling and slurping.

"Freak," Stetler spat. He sloped away, toward a new group of kids.

I knew it wasn't over. I knew Stetler wouldn't let me onto the bus without paying. But what could I do?

Darius and I spent the next minute picking Cine-Blocks off the asphalt and grass. There must have been hundreds of pieces. No, *thousands.*

"This is a disaster," I moaned. "Half our blocks are destroyed. How are we going to film the close-up scenes now?"

"No sweat," said Darius. "It just means more scenes for the real *Creeposaurus rex.* Those are better, anyway. They have people in them. *Girls.*" Darius wiggled his eyebrows.

Oh man.

Do you remember that thing I mentioned earlier? The *other* reason that Darius cast me in the leading-man, Hollywood-heartthrob role?

This was it.

My stomach lurched. I felt all kinds of bugs in it, crawling around.

"You asked her, right?" Darius whispered. "She said she'd act in the movie?"

I scooped up a Cine-Block.

"C'mon, Arlo, of course she'll say yes. She's, like, your best friend since forever!"

"Not forever," I mumbled.

Darius's eyes suddenly flicked up the street. Not the street where we'd walked from. The other street.

No. The driveway across from my house.

"Kayla! Hey, Kayla!" His bullfrog voice shouted. "Over here! Arlo wants to ask you something!"

My heart shrank. The rest of my bones disappeared.

I wanted to curl up and die.

Kayla Caine is my neighbor. She's also the nicest, prettiest, most untouchable girl in my neighborhood, high school included.

Kayla's hair is silver like fleece. She has dark eyebrows to match her dark eyes, plus a perfect-sized nose. She has perfect-sized *everything*.

SLLLRRRPP!

There was a sloshing noise as my knees buckled. I felt my whole body sink toward the sidewalk.

Kayla Caine and I were best friends growing up. That part is true. In our closet at home, Mom has four full-sized albums with nothing but pictures of Kayla and me. In our yards. At fancy restaurants. Even at Myrtle Beach, for vacation.

When strangers see those albums, the first thing they say (apart from "Arlo, where are your bones?") is, "Your daughter looks just like an angel, Mrs. Vreeland."

Mom laughs and corrects them. "Oh no, that's just Kayla. Arlo's *very special* friend." She waggles her eyebrows and everything.

Which is typical Mom. So embarrassing. But also so out of date. And just wrong.

As time passed, I got weirder and weirder, while Kayla got smarter and taller and prettier. No wonder we stopped hanging out.

Fourth grade changed everything. Fifth grade cemented things. Now, in sixth grade, the gap between Kayla and me was…colossal.

Like the Grand Canyon. Like *oceans*.

Darius just can't understand that.

"OOOF!" I uttered a gasp as someone shoved me aside. My legs slurped and I flopped to the street like an overcooked noodle.

Anger flashed in my eyes. Darius? Was it Darius?

No. It was Stetler! His tanklike body rushed forward, knocking people aside—almost shaking the street—as he charged up to Kayla.

Her pretty eyes stretched. *"C-Craig?"*

"Kayla! Yo!" Stetler slid to a stop, like an acrobat-elephant. "'Sup K? Get my text?"

Then he did something crazy. He hugged her! They walked the rest of the way arm-in-arm.

I couldn't believe it. Stetler? Craig Stetler?

And Kayla?

I barely heard the bus when it screeched to a halt at the curb. I was too shocked. I felt like a puddle of mud someone stepped on.

"Arlo, c'mon." Darius hauled me onto my ankles.

Everyone pushed toward the bus. At the very top step, Stetler paused. He cast an evil grin over his shoulder. I felt his shark-like eyes fix on me, even as Kayla was pulling him back.

"Later," he mouthed.

His finger slashed a line on his throat.

"You're dead meat."

6

"WOW, DR. VREELAND! You did it! You saved me!"

"You're the bravest person I ever met, Dr. Vreeland!"

"Kiss me, you wonderful man!"

Darius recited his lines in a squeaky and rat-like falsetto. We were in back of the bus, reading parts of the movie script off our phone screens.

My cheeks turned as bright as tomatoes. "Darius, no offense, but this dialogue stinks."

"It'll sound better when Kayla says it."

"Not so loud!" I hissed. "And no, I don't think it will."

Darius shrugged. "Keep reading. We're almost at the part with the Creeps!" A manic gleam crossed his eyes.

We spent the rest of the ride discussing the action scenes. Darius had every big moment mapped out. Entering the museum. Rushing through corridors. Confronting the Creeps—a.k.a. the zombie *Creeposaurus rex* skeletons that were supposed to chase us across the museum.

If Darius ever makes it to Hollywood, it'll be for his action scenes. He's got real talent. Plus he can actually *do* the effects. He's a wizard with Final Cut Pro.

Too bad he's such a turkey at writing. But I knew we could change the lines later.

Movie people have a saying, which is, "Don't worry, we'll fix it in post." Post stands for post-production. It means you can flub a scene during filming, but still fix it up afterward.

I hoped the saying was true, because our script was a mess. *And we're still short an actress,* I thought miserably.

I felt a quiver of fear. I could already see Kayla rejecting me. When that happened, wouldn't it be Darius's squeaky voice playing Dr. Hannah Yacob and wanting to kiss me?

Can you imagine? Can you *really* imagine?

Darius wasn't half as worried as I was.

"It's perfect," he said, closing the script file. "Once we wrap, they'll have to let us into the Shudder Oaks Film Festival. *And we'll win.* We'll be the talk of the town!"

"Yeah, sure," I mumbled.

My eyes drifted up the aisle to where Kayla was sitting. Her perfect lips curled in a smile that stretched to her ears.

And who was she smiling at? Stetler.

My skin prickled. My heart almost popped.

Just ask her, I begged myself. *Do it quick. Do it now.*

But I didn't. I couldn't.

I froze.

DARIUS AND I were last off the bus that morning.

"See you boys in an hour!" waved the driver. I didn't wave back. I was too focused on descending the steps without squishing and flopping.

My brain was a mess.

"Homeroom is *this* way," Darius laughed.

"Oh, duh."

We turned left toward Ms. Wellington's classroom. The entire sixth grade was supposed to check in for homeroom before walking back to the field trip bus.

Pointless, I know.

And I was so overwhelmed, thinking about Stetler and Kayla, and also about Uncle Leo, and the movie with Darius, and Dad's stupid bone diagrams, that I could hardly control myself. Even my fingers were trembling.

Finally, I unzipped my bookbag and pulled out Uncle Leo's bone invitation. I squeezed it tight like a stress ball.

A stress bone?

"DUDE!" Darius's loud voice erupted. "What IS that? What's in your HAND?"

His sneaker slid to a halt and he stared at the bone.

"*Arch-Archaeopteryx?*" I said, half-remembering. "Late Jurassic, I think. It's a fossil. Which one did you get?"

Darius gaped at me. I explained all about the fossil that clunked on my doorstep that morning. He was totally shocked. No, he hadn't gotten his own invitation. He hadn't heard of anyone else getting one, either. But what shocked him the most was the message engraved across the front.

"Special Forbidden Zone access," he read aloud. "Whoa, it's even personalized!" His eyes stretched like moons. "This is way cool, Arlo. Your uncle must be *completely insane* to use a fossil as a ticket stub!"

"You sound like my dad," I replied.

Darius's eyes twinkled. "Paging Dr. Fossil! Dr. Fossil!"

We both laughed.

"You really didn't get one?" I asked.

"Nope. Tell your uncle I'm totally jealous. That engraving is one of a kind."

One of a kind. My thoughts raced.

Was it true? Had Uncle Leo made the bone invitation for me? Only me?

I felt a rush of excitement. Of course he did! How many kids owned a real dinosaur fossil? I couldn't believe I'd shrugged it off before. I hadn't realized how rare this invitation was. Or how lucky I was to have Uncle Leo as part of the family.

"I wonder what the Forbidden Zone is," I said quietly.

"I don't know," said Darius, "but we are *definitely* checking it out."

We bumped fists. "Can't wait," I agreed.

"Nor can we, Mr. Vreeland."

Who said that? I spun around in alarm. A short woman with thick orange hair stepped into the hallway. Her portable laser light skipped past our eyes.

"Ms. Wellington!" we gasped.

Ms. Wellington's eyes didn't spark the way they normally did. She stowed her laser light without smiling once.

"Boys," she said solemnly. "I have some difficult news about today's field trip."

"Huh? What happened?"

"Why don't you both come inside?"

Darius and I followed Ms. Wellington through the open doorway and into her classroom. Everyone else was seated already. No one spoke or looked up at us. Not even Stetler. His shark-like eyes were fixed on the projector screen, same as the others.

A *Triosset Tribune* article beamed across the whiteboard.

JURASSIC LARK!

Ditzy Director Loses Dubious Dino

Surprise, surprise: Mr. Leonard Vreeland, embattled director of Triosset's so-called 'Museum of Natural History', has flubbed his lines once again. Known for his eccentric taste and near-complete lack of credentials, Director Vreeland has faced criticism across the scientific community for his alleged discovery of the *Creeposaurus rex*, a new dinosaur species. Experts, including his own brother, the esteemed Dr. Harold Vreeland of Cretaceia College, argue the 'Creeposaurus' is, in fact, a chimaera: a blend of existing, known fossils, incorrectly assembled. But now the truth may no longer be relevant, as the forty-foot skeleton of doubtful origin was reported stolen this morning. According to Director Vreeland, it disappeared from its perch and has yet to be found. Police are laughing and searching the scene…

[Click *NEXT* to read more; but first, a series of high-volume, unblockable ads from our sponsor!]

My mouth fell open. Darius and I traded thunderstruck looks.

"Uncle Leo!"

"The Creeposaurus rex!"

"It's…it's…"

Ms. Wellington frowned at us.

"Gone," she said quietly.

7

AS SOON AS THE PROJECTOR clicked off, the whole class erupted.

"Crazy! Just crazy!"

"How do you lose a forty-foot skeleton?"

"What kind of doofus could do that?"

Craig Stetler pounded his desk. "Vreeland! The doofus's last name was Vreeland!" He started laughing hysterically.

"Quiet, please!" Ms. Wellington's laser light stabbed across Stetler's face. It was an eye-safe laser, unfortunately, so it couldn't do damage. But she *had* switched the laser design onto "Clown Face."

Which I really enjoyed.

"Can we still go to the museum?" Darius asked. "We won't have to stay here and...*do math*, right?"

His eyes flicked toward the homework bin.

"Oh, the *horror.*" Ms. Wellington pretended to shudder. "The truth is, even I do not know the answer. Normally, I would expect our trip to be canceled. However, the current museum director is...unpredictable. And I know for a fact he is very interested in your attendance today. *Very* interested."

28

My eyes scrunched. So Uncle Leo *did* have something planned for us...

Ms. Wellington's phone beeped and she glanced at the screen. "Oh thank goodness!" she said after a moment. "The trip isn't canceled. We're going!"

Everyone cheered.

"Now just to be clear," said Ms. Wellington, reading more of the message, "there will be changes to our normal routine. As we speak, the police are investigating. There is an active crime scene inside the museum—perhaps more than one—and certain exhibits are completely off limits. In order for our trip to succeed, everyone has to be on their best behavior. Absolutely no monkey business. Okay?"

"Why are you looking at me?" Stetler sulked.

Excited whispers ran through the classroom. Darius and I traded looks. My mouth opened. I was ready to call it quits on the movie. It was too risky now that police might be hanging around.

Then I saw the glimmer in Darius's eye.

"This is gonna be *great*," he whispered.

I blinked at him. "You still want to film? What about our script? How can we do our scenes with police around? Caution tape? A missing *Creeposaurus rex* skeleton?"

"New movie," said Darius. "Dr. Arlo Vreeland and...and the Lost Creeposaurus! A documentary adventure. No, a thriller! A shaky-cam, found-footage horror!"

Excitement blazed in his eyes. Behind them, I could see the wheels in his head turning.

Darius can improvise *anything*.

Against my better judgment, I started feeling excited again. My heart buzzed. I couldn't wait to start filming.

Also, I wanted to see Uncle Leo. I wanted to make sure he was okay. Had he read that dumb article? Maybe Darius and I could help him investigate the crime scene. Dad's bone diagrams would have to wait, clearly.

Or maybe not. What if Darius and I somehow found the missing *Creeposaurus rex* skeleton? Imagine how famous we'd be then!

Kid heroes. Town legends.

Not even Kayla Caine could say no to a legend.

FIVE MINUTES LATER, our entire class filed out the door and into the hallway. Everyone was joking and laughing and discussing the incident. Stetler didn't even punch anyone (that I noticed).

The line screeched to a halt just in front of the entrance. My shins squished and I almost flopped over. Thank God that I didn't. The lady blocking the exit would've probably killed me.

"Aaahh!" Ms. Wellington shrieked, before quickly recovering. "Ahem. Mrs. Fawcett. What a pleasant surprise."

Ms. Wellington brushed her orange hair awkwardly.

"Permission slips out!" Mrs. Fawcett demanded.

Mrs. Fawcett is probably the worst human being I know. She's basically a professional chaperone. She has a daughter who graduated, like, three years ago. You'd think she'd leave us alone. But she *doesn't*. She comes back every year to yell at kids during field trips and dances. Everyone pretty much hates her.

Darius rummaged through his bookbag. A clump of Cine-Blocks plonked to the floor, drawing Mrs. Fawcett's eye. Like the Grim Reaper, she stalked over.

"Here," Darius said nervously. He wiped a Cine-Block fang off his permission slip and handed it over.

Mrs. Fawcett's toady eyes stared at it.

"Passable," she snorted. *"And you?"*

My heart jolted. She was looking at me.

Did I have a permission slip? No. But only because I was specifically told not to bring one.

"I, uh…it's my uncle's museum," I stammered.

"No permission slip?" Mrs. Fawcett said nastily.

"I'm Arlo Vreeland," I explained. "My uncle is Leonard Vreeland, the museum director. He's the one who organized our trip. *He's* my permission slip."

Mrs. Fawcett's lips twitched. "Each student must present a permission slip signed by a parent or guardian," she recited. "I don't care if your uncle is Pope Francis with a direct line to God. He won't count!"

A laser light flashed on the wall. Ms. Wellington was shuffling over.

"It's, er, true, Mrs. Fawcett. Arlo's uncle really did put the trip together. That's why I told Arlo he wouldn't need a permission slip. It just didn't seem necessary."

"The law is the law, Ms. Wellington. I'm sure Principal Chillbody would agree." Mrs. Fawcett's bulbous eyes flashed. "You have a Performance Review coming up, do you not? Perhaps I'll put in a word. Would you like that?"

Ms. Wellington shook her head. She looked terrified.

That's when something truly horrible happened.

"I-I agree with Mrs. Fawcett," said a girl's shaky voice.

I spun around.

Kayla. It was Kayla!

"Arlo shouldn't be allowed to leave without a permission slip," Kayla said quietly. "It's not fair to the other students. And also, it's not...it's not safe."

My eyes nearly popped and fell out.

Not safe? NOT SAFE?

Kayla wouldn't look at me. Her dark eyes glanced at Stetler. I heard the soft slap of their palms connecting—*a high five?!*—as Mrs. Fawcett gripped my shoulders and led me away like a criminal.

"Enjoy school," Stetler called after me. *"Freak!"*

TEN MINUTES LATER...

"One-two-three! One-two-three! Keep pulling! No pain, no gain, people!"

That awful voice belonged to Mr. Smithers, our substitute gym teacher. He was stalking around the gymnasium, spreading doom, gloom and pinecone cologne. I nearly gagged as I eyed the pull-up bar in front of me.

How had I gotten here? How did this happen?

I glanced around the room, at all the minuscule bodies surrounding me.

First graders. Six-year-olds!

"Excuse me, Mr. Smithers?" I said. "This isn't my class. Someone brought me here by mistake."

Mrs. Fawcett, I thought coldly.

"Less talking, more pull-ups!" said Mr. Smithers. "Work those noodles, boy!"

He swept over to where I was standing. Then, like a human pine tree, he lifted me onto the pull-up bar.

"Don't jump off," said Mr. Smithers. He turned to go.

THUMP! My feet hit the floor again.

Mr. Smithers whirled on me. "What did I say, boy? Don't jump off of the...the..."

Mr. Smithers's voice trailed away. I could tell by his shocked expression that he'd noticed what happened.

I *hadn't* let go of the pull-up bar. I'd just sort of...stretched. My boneless arms sagged toward the floor like a pair of bungee cords covered in hair. Finally, I released the bar and stepped backward.

Mr. Smithers's blocklike jaw dropped. He stared in horror and shock as my arms slowly shrank back to size.

"Gallopin' Grandpappies, boy! Where are your BONES?"

I stared at him.

"N-Nurse's office!" he stammered. "R-Right away!"

I squished my way out of there. Fast. As the gymnasium door slammed behind me, I breathed a sigh of relief.

Free. I was free. So now what?

Was I really going to deliver myself to Nurse Chang's office? Are you crazy? Do you have any idea how uncomfortable of a place that is for me? I'm not somebody's lab rat. I don't need my arms poked and prodded.

No thank you.

I was still walking, kind of aimlessly, when something flashed in a window. There was a deafening roar from outside.

The Creeposaurus rex, I thought crazily.

I pressed my nose to the glass. *Of course* it wasn't a world-famous dinosaur skeleton. But it was probably the *next* coolest thing.

"A charter bus," I whispered. *A private bus for our trip!*

I turned my ear toward the half-open window.

"Now this is more like it!" said our regular bus driver. "Heated seats! Closed circuit television! There's even a George Foreman grill in the back!"

"Is there a bathroom?" Mrs. Fawcett demanded. She clutched her soft, toadlike belly. There was a gurgle so loud, even *I* heard it.

"Er, yes," said the driver. "In the back. *The very back.*"

"Outta my way." Mrs. Fawcett pushed toward the bus. No one argued.

"Bookbags in here," Ms. Wellington announced. Her laser light stabbed at the bus, where a vast luggage compartment sprang open. "Yes, even yours, Mr. Moreland," she added.

Darius's smile flickered. With extreme reluctance, he tucked his blue Jansport bookbag in one of the corners. It was immediately crunched by a million more bookbags and purses and satchels until almost no space remained. Just a gap about as wide as a kneecap.

"My bookbag…can't fit…" someone puffed.

"I got you, fam." Out of nowhere, Stetler rushed up and rammed the bookbags. There was a sickening CRUNCH! as the last one squeezed in.

"That's it," said Ms. Wellington. "Everything fits. Whew. There's no room at all! You'd need bones made of Jello to fit inside now. Ahem. Books. I meant *books* made of—oh, nevermind."

She disappeared up the charter bus steps.

So did everyone else.

I felt my skin tingle. A fire lit in my eyes as I thought, *What would Uncle Leo do in this situation? What would Darius do? No. What would Dr. Arlo Vreeland, the next Indiana Jones, choose to do?*

My chest fluttered. Quick as water, I splashed up the hall toward the exit. I slurped through the double glass doors.

And I *ran* for that bus.

My bones squished, churned and flopped. I ignored them. I reached the luggage compartment at a run, just as the last student climbed up the steps. No one watched as I squeezed into place, like a huge wad of Play-Doh. A second later, the driver came out to inspect the compartment.

"All clear," he said without looking.

The luggage door slammed. The bus roared.

We were off!

TWO MINUTES LATER, the bus driver's voice crackled over the intercom.

"Wow. Haha. Is this charter bus bumpy or what? There seems to be a—" *KA-THUMP!* "—loose tire somewhere! Never fear, we'll be arriving in—" *KA-KA-THUMPPP!* "—thirty short minutes. Hang on!"

Loud voices screamed through the aisles.

"Can't...breathe..." I gasped, between two hulking bookbags.

How cramped was I?

Sardine-style cramped. Opening night of *Spider-Man* cramped. I felt like tuna fish stuffed in a can.

Desperate for air, I wriggled deeper into the compartment. The bus was shaking all over, causing all kinds of slurps in my bones, which I cringed and ignored. Finally, I found a spot I could breathe in.

Some kind of air pipe. A vent.

Like a surfacing scuba diver, I poked my head up and took huge, gasping breaths. I breathed until all the air in that pipe got sucked out.

"Oh thank God," I said.

I leaned my head on the pipe, letting my arms and legs slump. The lack of oxygen left me sleepy and I must've dozed off, because next I remember, a woman's voice woke me up.

"Bathroom," it groaned. "E-Emergency! Step aside!"

"Are you all right, Mrs. Fawcett? You look...*green.*"

"MOVE IT, SHRIMP!"

Heavy footsteps shook the cabin above me. A door opened. A lid slammed. And out came a sound like Mount St. Helens, an active volcano, erupting.

BLRRRGGBBGHGHHHFFF!

My eyelids fluttered. My nose crinkled, then shriveled and died, as a gust of air whooshed through the pipe. I started choking at once.

"Ohhhh sick!" I cried. *"Ohhh nnoooo!"*

It was the foulest smell in the universe. The absolute nastiest stench in the world! I felt my *insides* turning inside out. I wanted to die.

Where was I hiding? Where was I crazily sucking down air? Inside of a pipe connected to the charter bus bathroom.

"Ahhhhhhhhh," Mrs. Fawcett moaned from above.

There was another foul blast of air.

Then another.

9

ASK ANY MOVIE PERSON and they'll tell you: there are good and bad ways to die. Suffocation by toxic poop gas is one of the worst.

How long was I trapped for? It was over ten minutes. Way over.

I want to stress how disgusting it was. When I finally pulled free and got off of that bus, I was a different person. A worse person. My life force was permanently weakened.

So next time you think your life is going sideways and all hope is lost, think of me. Think of your boy, Arlo, and the pipe I was forced to inhale from.

I could taste it, you know.

When the air gets that thick, there's a taste.

Have a nice rest of your day.

MY EYES LEAKED like faucets and I couldn't stop gagging. Nothing I did seemed to work. No amount of grunting and squeezing could force me out of that pipe until, suddenly, the entire bus screamed out in terror.

The luggage compartment and everything in it lurched sideways, including myself.

"Aaaaaahhhh!" shrieked the bus driver. "D-D-Dinosaur!"

We did a three-sixty spin in the parking lot. There were all sorts of rumbles and squeaks as our wheels popped the curb. Then a big, bullfrog voice shouted, "Creeposaurus! Yo, it's the missing Creep bones! We're heading straight for the—"

CRRRRRNNNNNCCCHHHHHH!

There was the sickening sound of snapped bone. Our charter bus squealed to a halt on the sidewalk in front of Uncle Leo's museum.

"WELCOME TO THE MUSEUM OF NATURAL HISTORY!" said a big, bone-white sign. It was still standing, thank God.

The ten-foot-tall *Creeposaurus rex* sculpture was *not*. Its many, many bones lay in pieces across the sidewalk. Stiff, yellow pieces. Up close, they looked like bits of uncooked spaghetti.

Would you believe it if I told you they *were* bits of uncooked spaghetti?

"Foiled again," sighed the sculptor. "The timing is never quite right for my art!" He scooped a pair of stiff noodles into his pocket, sniffed once, then trod away, scowling.

Guess how I knew that?

Because the luggage compartment sprang open! I was catapulted across the sidewalk along with the luggage. *Of course* I landed in a minefield of noodles. *Of course* that would happen.

My bones slurped like crazy as I rolled to my knees. A man wandered up to me. He was tall and lean, with bright eyes and a scruffy black beard. He also wore a black business suit, which is why I didn't instantly shout, "Uncle Leo!"

"I've always hated that statue," he laughed. "What kind of artist sculpts a dinosaur out of spaghetti? Clearly he should've used macaroni!"

Now I really did shout, "Uncle Leo!"

We traded big, goofy grins.

This is why I love Uncle Leo. He's so relaxed all the time. He didn't scold me or instantly panic. He just laughed and helped me onto my feet. We were both standing there, among the purses and bookbags, as the bus door swung open and my entire class tumbled out of it.

"Hey guys," I waved.

Darius let out a shriek in his rat-like falsetto.

"Arlo! Dude! HOW ARE YOU HERE?"

"Magic." I winked at him. The entire class followed my eyes to the massive stone-and-glass building beside us. *The Museum of Natural History.* Suddenly it didn't seem like such an exaggeration to call this place Hogwarts.

Yes. It looked a lot like a castle. There were arched windows and turrets and two enormous stone towers either side of the entrance. An eerie mist drifted between the upper floors, making me shiver.

Something about the building felt strange. Like it belonged somewhere else. Not in a tiny town like Triosset.

"What kind of stone is that?" Ms. Wellington asked. "I've never seen anything like it."

She pointed to the funky green-gray of the outer walls—the swirling red-brown of the towers—the strange lumps of yellow and white that were bulging across it—

"You're asking me," Uncle Leo laughed. "But who am I supposed to ask? I'm a museum director, not a scientist!" He laughed again. "But if I had to guess the material this museum is made of…"

His flashing eyes turned to me.

"Bones!" he cried out. "Hundreds and thousands of bones!"

His scruffy beard shook as he dissolved into cackling laughter. So did the rest of my class. Everyone found it hilarious. I told you, Uncle Leo is really charming. It's hard not to fall under his spell. He's less an adult than, like, a really big kid.

So how come I wasn't laughing? Why was my skin tingling? Why did my fuzzy red hair stand on end?

"Bones," I said quietly. Then I gulped and corrected myself. "Fossils."

The swirls on the walls. All those funky, impossible colors. They were fossils! Normal kids might not recognize them. But how could I not? How could the son of Dr. Harold Vreeland—a.k.a. Dr. Fossil—fail to identify a twenty-foot shale wall? Fossiliferous limestone?

A shiver ran through me. I suddenly had an impossible thought.

What if the entire museum, with its turrets and towers and creepy arched windows, hadn't really been built, but…exposed?

Chiseled out of the ground, like a fossil.

Like bone.

I was still staring, trying to puzzle things out, when a pale neck jutted out of the mist. For a split-second, I saw a massive, fanged skull with piercing red eyes.

My heart jolted. *A Creep! A Creeposaurus rex skull!*

The mist thickened and the dino skull vanished. I rubbed my eyes, feeling dizzy and a little bit stupid.

Whoa, I thought. *Am I crazy or what?*

Of course it wasn't a real *Creeposaurus rex* skull. *Of course* not.

Right?

I looked around to see if anyone else saw the skull. They hadn't. They were too busy staring in shock at the museum's front entrance.

The double doors had burst open. A clump of people were sprinting away at top speed as a thunderous noise shook the pavement.

RAWWWWWRRRRRR!

10.

POLICE OFFICERS. THEY WERE police officers! My jaw dropped as they crashed out the double glass doors, sprinting up the steps and across the spaghetti-strewn sidewalk.

These weren't rank-and-file 'donut' guys, either. This was SWAT. Special forces! Their heavy vests slapped their chins as they ran, and at least one of them carried a riot shield.

Half a riot shield. There was a vicious crack where the top had snapped off.

"BlaaaAAAaaaaaAaaaaaaaaaahhhhhh!" they screamed. "BLAAaaAAAaaaAAaWWgaH'NAGLLLFHTagGNn!!"

"Check out that howl," Darius whispered. "Doesn't it kind of remind you of CircleGirls?"

"Report in!" the police chief barked. "Did you find it? Did you encounter the target?"

The SWAT members exchanged nervous looks.

"W-With respect, sir, we don't know *what* we found."

"We swore never to speak of it!"

"E-Extinct. They're s-supposed to be extinct!"

They turned and fled for the parking lot.

Uncle Leo sauntered up to the shell-shocked police chief.

"I did warn you the missing *Creeposaurus rex* was likely hiding inside the museum," he said lazily.

"Y-You claimed there was a thief on the loose!" roared the chief. "A stone-cold killer!"

Uncle Leo shrugged.

"I should put you in handcuffs, Dr. Vreeland!"

"Please," said Uncle Leo. "It's *Mister* Vreeland. Doctor is for geeks, twerps and know-it-all younger brothers. Now if you don't mind," he said, yawning, "I'm terribly busy. I have tours to give. Skeletons to recapture! Or would you prefer to keep my nephew's sixth-grade class waiting outside in the cold?"

The police chief stomped his feet like an angry bull. His eyes flicked around, clearly looking for backup. There wasn't any. Not one other policeman was left.

Poor guy. I could see the wheels in his head turning. I wondered if he'd ever made a solo arrest before. Did he even own handcuffs? As chief of police, he probably spent most of his day in his office.

A long moment passed, followed by the sharp sound of noodles exploding. The police chief had made up his mind.

He'd fled for the parking lot.

IT TOOK US TEN MINUTES to get everything settled. Ms. Wellington, at least, was impressed that our trip was still on. Her laser light danced up the creepy bone walls, making me gasp a couple of times, thinking the *Creeposaurus rex* skull came back.

Guess how impressed Mrs. Fawcett was?

"No talking!" she barked.

"Step away from the steaming bus engine!"

"Drop the noodle, Erik! I don't care if the hot engine cooked it!"

Yes, our charter bus was a wreck. Half its tires sat on the sidewalk as steam piped from the hood. And where was our driver? Watching Netflix on the tiny TVs! We couldn't have left the museum if we wanted to.

I used the extra time to tell Darius about the *Creeposaurus rex* skull I'd seen in the tower.

"That's...perfect!" he exclaimed. "Now say it again, but with more grit this time." He held up his cell phone. Recording me.

I rolled my eyes. "I'm serious, Darius—"

"So am I, dude! Get your game face on. This movie is gonna be epic!"

"Okay, okay."

We shot the scene from a dozen more angles. When we finished, Darius waved me over and showed me some of his B-roll footage. Background scenes. Stuff like that.

We huddled around his phone screen, watching the SWAT members screaming and fleeing in terror.

Typical Darius. He'd been filming the whole time!

Finally, after what felt like an ice age, someone's hand squeezed my neck.

Uncle Leo, I thought, spinning round—

CLUNK!

And straight into a cold iron chestplate. My eyes bulged as I stared at the towering, seven-foot figure.

It was not Uncle Leo.

Metal screeched in my ears as a pair of rusty hands gripped my neck. Lifting me into the air. Dragging me toward the museum's main entrance.

Clomp. Clomp. Clomp.

Iron feet stomped the pavement. I tried to scream, but iron hands squeezed my windpipe. I couldn't breathe. Couldn't think.

I could only watch, horrified, as my reflection appeared in the museum's glass doors. I saw myself dangling in the arms of a monster. Something from the "Menacing Medieval Times" exhibit, or the movie *King Arthur.*

Yes. A seven-foot-tall suit of armor.

11

OKAY, I KNOW WHAT YOU'RE thinking. And it isn't just, "No way, Arlo, no way all that happened." It's also, like, "Whoa, hold up, what did *everyone else* do while this happened? Did Darius squeal like a rat? Did Ms. Wellington shoot her laser light? What about Kayla? Or Stetler? Or that brute, Mrs. Fawcett?"

This is why I have horrible luck. *No one was watching me.* Uncle Leo was giving a speech, introducing our class to the museum. Everyone's eyes were transfixed.

I saw it all in the door glass reflection. Uncle Leo's relaxed posture. His scruffy hair as he mussed it. And then, all the sudden, his eyebrows as they quivered and knitted together.

For a split-second, Uncle Leo and I locked eyes. *He saw me.* He saw the suit of armor that carried me off. *And he winked.*

SNAP!

I crashed through the doors and into the museum. I felt a heavy shove as I tipped forward and fell to the floor. My heart was beating like crazy. I could barely breathe as the suit of armor stood over me. It raised its rusty left boot. It was going to stomp me. To smash me.

"Noooooo!" I cried out. I started flailing my arms, trying anything I could think of. One of my hands hit the leg that was still planted on the floor. Frantic, I started crazily twisting and pulling it.

CLUNK!

A metal plate fell away, leaving a fist-sized hole in the armor. My eyes nearly popped when I stared through the gap. I don't know what I expected to see underneath the armor. Skin or something? A pant leg?

Not bone. Not a slimy brown bone!

"Aaaaahhhh!" I let out a horrified moan.

My whole body panicked. Too frightened to think, I went back to my original plan. I plunged a hand through the gap and started squeezing the bone. I tried to rip it away. To make the suit of armor tip over.

"Aaaaaahhhh!" I cried again.

Frostbite chewed through my fingers. The bone felt so slimy and cold. *Don't let go,* I begged myself. *Don't give up. Don't stop pulling!*

Icy chills shot up my fingers and wrists. I clenched my teeth and ignored them. I knew I couldn't stop pulling. I had to knock my attacker off balance before that rusty boot stomped me. Dislodging that creepy brown bone was my last chance—my only hope to survive!

But what if I told you I *didn't* survive?

My hand slipped. The rusty boot dropped on my chest like a stone.

There was a single loud SQUISH!

And then nothing.

12

THAT'S HOW MS. WELLINGTON and the other sixth-graders found me when they entered the museum. They didn't find Arlo, the nice, normal kid. They found Arlo the Freak, peeling himself up off the floor like a sponge someone stepped on.

"Waaaahhhhh!" Erik screamed.

"Freak," spat a voice (probably Stetler).

As I swayed to my feet, feeling nauseous, Kayla ran a finger through her silvery hair, then pointed it straight at my neck and cried, "Looook! Something's weird! What—what *is* it?"

My heart jolted. Had I lost a bone? Another bone?

I started frantically scratching my neck.

"No, Arlo, behind you!"

I spun around and saw a long line of slippery ooze. It began at my feet and drizzled halfway across the Entrance Hall. *And it was still moving.* Still crazily clicking and flopping on the cold tile floor.

Darius pointed his cell phone and beamed.

"Snake!" someone squealed. "It's a viper! A boa constrictor!"

No, it isn't, I thought. *It's the thing I pried loose from the suit of armor.*

A bone. Living bone.

I held my breath as it skipped down one of the corridors, out of sight.

SNAP! The museum doors banged open and Mrs. Fawcett came waddling in, clutching her huge belly.

"Ooof." Her toadlike eyes winced. "What'd I miss?"

WE WERE ALL PRETTY shaken up. Nevertheless, except for me, no one was sure what they'd seen. And guess again if you think people believe anything a boneless freak like me tells them.

Even Kayla was backtracking fast. She refused to meet my eye, which was extra annoying because there wasn't much time until filming began.

Darius was hot on my case.

"We *need* her, dude. Dr. Hannah Yacob has the biggest role in the film, next to yours!"

"I said I'd ask her," I grumbled. "Just give me a minute, okay? I was attacked by a big suit of armor. A zombie!"

"Not this again." Darius rolled his eyes. "Didn't we cut this scene already? It's too dumb for the movie."

"It's not a scene, Darius. It really happened!"

Darius sighed wearily. "Look, dude, I know you're trying to help. It's just, people expect Dr. Arlo Vreeland to be tougher than what you're describing. He can't go around getting stomped on by zombies. He's a hero, not a punching bag."

I shot him an icy look.

"Good, good!" Darius grinned. "You're finally getting in character!"

HAVE YOU EVER BEEN part of a group where you're the only one freaking out? Where everyone else is acting cool and collected and *completely* underestimating how much danger they're in?

That was me right now.

I guess it's always been me.

Because of my weird bones, and all the strange things I can do (like slip through one-inch gaps) and all the normal things I can't do at all (like sprint properly), people just kind of shrug and ignore me.

"Oh, that's just Arlo," they say. "He's a freak."

And when you're in a room with twenty-six other kids who all think everything is perfectly fine, and also think you're a freak for disagreeing with them, well, you start to doubt your own instincts. Even your own *memory*.

Was I really abducted by a zombie suit of armor?

Did I really see a red-eyed skull at the top of that tower?

I didn't know what to think. But with no proof either way, I tried to relax a little (just a little) and focus on making the movie with Darius.

As lead actor, I decided to do my very best hero impression. No more shrill screams or ankle-slurping. I was going to tromp through every part of the museum, including the scary parts, and give the greatest movie performance of all time (well, of all time for twelve-year-olds).

But that wasn't all, because I also had a hidden agenda.

To catch one of those freakazoid monsters on film.

To prove I wasn't a freak *or* a liar.

Guess what else? I already had a sneaking suspicion about what was happening. A suspicion so nuts, I couldn't say it out loud, not even to Darius.

Here goes:

The bones in this museum were alive. They could *move*.

13

BEFORE OUR CLASS LEFT the Entrance Hall, Darius dragged me across the floor to the edge of what looked like a massive exhibit. There was a glass pedestal in front, which had some kind of writing inside, plus a ring of bee-yellow tape that surrounded it all.

That tape looks kind of flimsy, I thought randomly.

As I stepped closer, I understood why.

It was police tape. The kind you find at a crime scene.

Darius jerked his head toward the pedestal. I followed his gaze to the large copper plaque inside.

SPECIES: *CREEPOSAURUS REX*
YEARS ACTIVE: 100 million BC – ???
HEIGHT: TALL
WEIGHT: HEAVY
DIET: OSSIVOROUS

My eyebrows crinkled. "Siri," I said aloud, "define 'Ossivorous.'"

My phone beeped and said, "Ossivorous. Adjective. Definition: Bone-eating, or given to chewing on bones."

Bone-eating!

I stared at the plaque. There was an informational note at the bottom.

> The *Creeposaurus rex* is a master of camouflage. This creature absorbs the bones of its prey, using them as part of its body. Possibly. We can't really know.
>
> — Leonard Vreeland, Author, "Things I Mostly Made Up."

"WHAT!" I cried out.

The rest of my class crowded round. They squinted down at the plaque.

"So the *Creeposaurus rex* used to be standing right here in the Entrance Hall?" someone said.

"I wonder who stole it? I heard the whole museum staff is out looking for it. That's why this place is so empty."

"Isn't this the room those police officers came running out of?" said a worried voice. "Do you think they saw the *Creeposaurus rex* skeleton? What if it came back and scared them away?"

"Yeah, sure. The *Creeposaurus rex* got up for a morning stroll. That explains it." Stetler barked out a laugh. "You're crazy if you believe anything the Ditzy Director wrote on that plaque. He's not a scientist. He's just randomly making things up."

Nervous laughter ran through the crowd. I opened my mouth to defend Uncle Leo, but then I remembered the title of the book he quoted: *Things I Mostly Made Up.*

Finally, the crowd split apart. I heaved a sigh of relief. I waited until even Stetler had lumbered off, then I leapt into action. I ducked beneath the police tape and entered the *Creeposaurus rex* exhibit.

Yes.

Darius shot me a thumbs-up. Of course he was filming me.

My heart pounded. I was even more scared than I expected. I knew I shouldn't be trespassing like this. You aren't supposed to walk inside of museum exhibits, especially ones with police tape.

On the other hand, I thought Uncle Leo would appreciate what I was doing.

Being adventurous. Filming a movie.

Uncle Leo is probably the craziest person I know. He's also a bit of a rebel. So I figured my character, Dr. Arlo Vreeland, should have a wild streak, too. Darius was right. I needed to start acting like a hero, not a punching bag.

Darius skirted around the police tape, filming from all different angles. He had me say a few random lines, like, "This isn't where I parked my car," or, "This is bad...super bad!"

I'm going to be honest. My acting wasn't the best. Breaking into an active crime scene had rattled my nerves.

"It's fine," Darius assured me. "We'll fix it in post-production."

That's what I said, I thought privately.

Out loud, I just groaned. I couldn't wait to get out of there.

For our last shot, I bent down and pretended to examine the floor. I gripped a strange hunk of brownish-gray rock I found laying there.

Weird.

The rock kind of looked like a starfish. I flipped it over. Not a starfish. A bone.

I drew a long, shaky breath as I stared at its five crumbly fingers.

"Human," I whispered. "It's human!"

14

A HUMAN HAND. A frail, shrunken, mummified hand! It felt so dry. As if all the thickness and life was sucked out of it. I gasped as it crumbled to dust in my fingers.

Darius lowered his camera. "Nice ad lib, dude! A human hand? Beats what I had in the script."

"It wasn't an ad lib," I spluttered. "D-Did you see it?"

"See what? I was filming."

"Check the film!"

But Darius wasn't listening. He was on another planet already. Spielberg planet. The land of directors.

"The missing *Creeposaurus rex* has returned," he announced, in a movie-trailer-type voice. "Its bony body is terrorizing the museum-goers. It's on a rampage! Can Dr. Arlo Vreeland follow the clues to its lair and retrieve the, er…sacred artifact that powers its sick zombie magic?"

Darius beamed after pitching his movie.

That's a pretty good plot, I thought randomly.

Then my thoughts splintered. I stared at the mummified dust in my hand. Then I freaked out and flung it aside, storming out of the exhibit. I couldn't believe what just happened.

I'm going crazy, I thought. *I really am going crazy.*

Darius pressed me for details. "So what was it, really? A Cine-Block? It couldn't have been a Creep bone."

"It was a hand, Darius. I'm not joking."

Darius still didn't believe me. "Decent idea, though. Do you think the real *Creeposaurus rex* hunted humans? Human bones, I mean?"

"Humans didn't *exist* in the dinosaur era," I reminded him.

"You sure?"

I rolled my eyes. "You really need to start doing homework."

Darius laughed. He unzipped his bookbag and started pulling out Cine-Blocks. Because of Stetler, our *Creeposaurus rex* models were totally wrecked. So why was Darius dumping them onto the floor like loose bones?

"Trust me, Arlo. This is gonna look great in the lens. Like a boneyard!"

He dropped to his knees, filming everything. I peered around. It was fine. No one was watching us.

So how come a shiver ran through me?

Why were there chills down my neck?

I started checking the rafters. The staircase. The second-floor railing that loomed like a shadow above us.

All the sudden, my blood froze. A pair of piercing red eyes lifted out of the gloom. I felt my jaw drop as my whole body trembled. No, I didn't see the Creeposaurus's fangs this time. I didn't need to.

It ROARED.

15

RAAWWWWRRRRR!!!!

The noise shook through the empty museum. Dust fell from the second-floor railing, quickly followed by something else.

Something huge.

I grabbed Darius by his blue Jansport bookbag and hauled him away—barely—as a massive object SPLAT-TERED the place where he stood. There was a violent CRAAACK! as the tile floor ripped apart, sending Cine-Blocks flying like shrapnel.

Darius let out a shriek. So did I. So did everyone.

My entire class stood and stared at the enormous, gray-and-brown skull that had crushed the *Creeposaurus rex* exhibit.

It was a dinosaur skull. Brontosaurus? Brachiosaurus? One of the plant-eaters, surely. A strip of spine was still fused to the bottom. There was a nasty crack underneath, where the spine bone had severed.

My blood chilled.

It looked totally sick. Like a bite mark.

Everyone was freaking out. Kayla turned pale as a ghost. Even Stetler was shaking. The only person who wasn't afraid was Erik Stotz. He took a giant step forward.

"Don't go near it!" I blurted out. "There's something wrong with these fossils. They MOVE!"

Erik slid to a halt, looking skeptical. I waited for the skull to do something. I felt sure that it would.

Would its eyes glow bright red? Would it leap away like the shin bone I'd wrestled?

The seconds ticked by. Nothing happened.

By now a lot of kids were eyeing me strangely. Stetler snapped out of his daze and waddled up to the skull. He flashed me an evil glare— *"This could be you,"* it meant—as he thumped the skull with his toe.

CRRRNCCHH!!! Its jaw fell apart like a piece of burned toast.

Dry, I thought crazily. *Something sucked the skull dry!*

"Craig Stetler!" Ms. Wellington scolded. "What on Earth are you doing? Get back here!"

"Sorry, Ms. Welly. Freak said the skull was alive, so I wanted to check."

"We don't call people names, Craig!"

"Sorry, Ms. Welly—I mean, Ms. Wellingto—OHH!!"

Stetler broke off in a moan. Eyes wide, he scrambled backward and hid behind Kayla. His shaky hand pointed back at the skull.

We all watched it.

It moved.

16

DEAD SILENCE. The giant skull shook like an egg as something squeezed through the cracks.

My jaw dropped.

A living bone. Another hand bone!

First the left hand crawled out, then the right. I'd never seen anything so foul and disgusting. My breath caught in my throat. I nearly gagged. The hand bones rushed toward us with shocking speed, crawling on tiny, gray fingers.

Wait. No. They were feet.

Ms. Wellington let out a wail. "RATS! THOSE ARE RATS!"

The rats sped past our ankles. I let out a wild breath.

"Rats," I muttered. "Not living fossils. Just rats."

If they really were rats, I thought crazily. I tried to get a better look, but they were already gone.

By now kids were grinning and laughing. They thought the danger was over. As if the existence of rats explained everything.

"Rats can chew through cement," someone said. "Their tiny teeth are like knives. They could definitely bite off a fossil."

"Yeah," one of my classmates added. "Bet you those rats chewed a hole in that spine bone. That's why the skull hit the ground. Those rats are lucky they survived that huge fall!"

The rats are lucky? I thought. *The stinking rats?*

"No wonder the *Creeposaurus rex* went missing," Stetler chuckled. "This museum is infested with bone-eating rats!"

There were nods of agreement.

"Those rats probably scared the police officers."

"Exactly. And they scared us, too! Remember that thing Kayla saw? Bet you a million bucks it was a rat."

Mrs. Fawcett had a big scowl on her face. "Everyone form a single-file line behind me," she demanded. "This museum is a death trap. We are leaving this instant!"

Her giant hands gripped the double glass doors. She pulled until her pudgy cheeks turned bright red.

"Locked!" she cried out. "Firmly locked!"

Everyone rushed over. We took turns pulling the handles. Nothing happened. The doors wouldn't budge.

"Could it be a one-way door?" said Ms. Wellington. "Maybe there's a separate exit in back of the museum?"

Mrs. Fawcett glared at her. "Impossible! That's a fire code violation. It's against the law to build a door like that!" She stamped her feet angrily.

Meanwhile, Ms. Wellington was drifting deeper into the museum. There was an excited gleam in her eyes.

Like I said before, Ms. Wellington is a great teacher. She's always up for adventure. She doesn't mind bending the rules, either.

"Well then," she said with a clap of her hands, "there's no use crying over spilled fossils. It seems the only way OUT of this museum…is to go DEEPER IN!"

Ms. Wellington did an about-face, like an army sergeant, and marched us to the back of the Entrance Hall. Dozens of dark corridors were branching off it, like the multiple paths of a maze.

"Flashlight apps out, everyone! It's time to explore!"

GUESS WHO LAGGED BEHIND the rest of his class? My joints sloshed around like cold soup. I had a lot on my mind. Maybe that's why the strange silver flash got the jump on me.

"Aahhh!" I yelled. My shins slurped as I stumbled around.

Was it a living bone? Another zombie suit of armor? Either one would've made more sense than what actually reached out and grabbed me.

"Kayla!" I gasped.

Kayla reached a hand out to steady me. Her silver hair splashed down her face and into my eyes.

"You need to walk faster, Arlo," she warned me. "Stay close to the group and don't fall behind. It's not safe for you to be alone here."

I stared at her. I thought back to how Kayla had almost gotten me banned from the trip. It suddenly made sense.

"Did Stetler say something?" I asked. "Does he still want to hurt me?"

Kayla's dark eyebrows shifted.

"You don't need to protect me," I grumbled. "I can handle Stetler just fine on my own."

"Stetler isn't who I'm worried about," said Kayla. "Please, Arlo, take my advice." She squeezed my arm before releasing me and walking away.

I watched her go with pursed lips. Yes, I was mad. Mad and embarrassed. But I was also a little bit dazed. Kayla's Pearberry body spray hung in the air, making my heart flutter.

I felt a sudden burst of inspiration. "Hey Kayla!" I blurted out. "Do you, um, want to be in a movie with me?"

I eyed the back of her silver head hopefully. Did she hear what I said? Would she do it?

No answer.

"Yo, dude!" Darius came scurrying up to me. "I saw you two talking and—"

I cut him off with a head shake. "She didn't say yes. But she didn't say no, either," I added hopefully.

I was expecting Darius to grumble or utter a curse, so I was surprised to see him still smiling.

"Bah, we'll win her over eventually."

He clapped a hand on my shoulder. I suddenly noticed how excited he was. He kept peering down at his phone screen, then up at the empty museum. His eyes had that faraway, Spielberg-type look again.

"We're going to do great things in this museum, Arlo," he said finally. "Terrible, oh yes. But GREAT!"

He laughed wickedly.

Yes. I know it's a line from the first *Harry Potter* movie. One of Darius's all-time favorites.

Was it true, though? Was Darius right?

What if I told you I just spent five minutes trying to think of a better summary sentence and failed?

Great and terrible things.

That's exactly what our class trip was in for.

17

DARIUS AND I HUNG BACK as the rest our class grouped around a large wooden signpost in back of the Hall.

"Hmm," said Ms. Wellington. "Decisions, decisions!"

She peered at the signpost. A dozen arrows pointed every direction, each leading down a different dark corridor that twisted and turned out of sight.

My skin prickled. I couldn't believe how many corridors there were. And why were they so dark? How come you couldn't see anything? Suddenly Uncle Leo's museum felt like one giant maze.

Or a cave system. Or the bowels of a castle.

"Oh, these names are exciting!" said Ms. Wellington. "Shall we begin with the Egyptian Horrors exhibit? Ancient Greek Warfare? Or what about dinosaurs? There are three separate fossil rooms: Triassic Park, Jurassic Pagoda and...oh my goodness!"

Her brown eyes suddenly lit up like torches. "The Sorcerer's Tomb," she read aloud. "Mmm! Spooky!"

At these words, a gust of wind suddenly stirred out of nowhere. There were loud creaks as the wooden signpost spun around like a top.

"G-Ghost!" Erik squealed.

Several kids laughed. By then the signpost had stopped spinning. All the arrows were pointing in random directions.

Ms. Wellington's grin could have lit up a tunnel. "I wonder how many times this signpost has spun around?" she mused. "Do *any* of these arrows mean anything?"

It was obvious she didn't mind not knowing where the corridors led. She might've even preferred it.

"Let me see that!" Mrs. Fawcett plowed forward, clutching her belly. "Restroom," she growled. "I need the sign for the restroom."

"Aieeee!" I let out a squeak as Darius pinched me.

He pointed to the trail of slippery ooze left behind by the bone that attacked me.

"It's got great visuals," he whispered. "I'll film you walking behind it. C'mon!"

I took one look at the slime trail and shuddered. I turned away in disgust.

Darius saw me and laughed. "Relax, dude. You're still worried about the rat?"

"It wasn't a rat," I hissed. "It was a bone. A living bone!"

Darius wasn't listening. His dark eyes bulged as he stared past my shoulder at the slippery slime trail.

"I don't believe it," he whispered.

I spun around and saw a lock of silvery hair whip round the bend, followed by the huge, tree-trunk legs of Craig Stetler.

My mouth fell open. "K-Kayla?" I spluttered.

Darius filmed her last, careful steps and sighed airily. "She's got guts, dude. And star power! She'll be a huge hit in the movie."

"She never agreed to do the movie," I reminded him.

"Too late," said Darius. "She's already in it." He stowed his cell phone and grinned.

My thoughts raced. Why was Kayla sneaking off to follow the slime trail? Did she have any idea how dangerous that bone creature was? And why go with Stetler? Since when did they start hanging out?

I turned to Darius. I could tell we were both thinking the same thing.

Should we follow them?

We were still standing there when a greasy hand clapped our shoulders.

"No dawdling! The Sorcerer's Tomb is this way."

Mrs. Fawcett dragged us down the opposite corridor, away from the slime. Away from Kayla and Stetler. Except for Darius and me, no one had seen them sneak off.

They were gone.

1.8

IT WAS SCARIER THAN I expected. The corridor we explored had no lights, so everyone bumped elbows and staggered around. We were all crammed together. Every breath felt like gasping. A couple times I almost squished and fell down. Only the fear of being trampled on in the dark kept my shins from collapsing.

I didn't want to die like that.

I couldn't.

I was Dr. Arlo Vreeland, the famous explorer. How could I die in a freak way like that?

Ms. Wellington's pace quickened. Her laser light glanced off the chilly stone walls, barely illuminating anything. Thankfully, our cell phone flashlights were better.

"Dude, check it out!"

Dark shadows scampered like rats as Darius aimed his light at the wall. My eyes widened. The corridor wasn't empty. It was packed wall to wall with exhibits! Mostly paintings in dusty brown frames.

"That can't be…a Picasso?" Mrs. Fawcett gasped.

She made Darius shine his light on a strange, cube-like painting. Then she grabbed us both by the neck, marching us up the corridor like human flashlights.

"Van Gogh! This is Vincent Van Gogh!"

"El Greco! El Greco!"

Mrs. Fawcett clutched her gurgling stomach. "This is a crime against art!" she exclaimed. "These paintings deserve their own private restroom—er, viewing room. Preferably with locked doors and heated seats. What kind of *madman* would leave them out in the dark?"

She glared at me, as if *I* knew the answer.

"Er, Uncle Leo likes scary stuff best," I said. "Bones. Mummies. He thinks they make a bigger impression."

It was something I'd heard my dad say before. And it seemed about right. I thought about the bone invitation Uncle Leo had sent me this morning. *That* had made an impression, all right.

"Your uncle is a grade A nitwit," Mrs. Fawcett declared.

For the record, I disagree with her.

Paintings attract a lot of publicity, but they're pretty lame in the end. I wasn't shocked that Uncle Leo ditched them in some random spot to make room for his fossils. You can't look straight up at a painting's huge head. You can't walk in circles around a painting, or secretly reach out and touch its spiked tail.

They also don't move, I thought, shivering.

"Over here!" said a voice. "I think I found something!"

"Is it the Sorcerer's Tomb? Are we there?"

Cell phone lights sliced through the dark. As people rushed forward, there was an echoing CLUNK!

"Aaaahhh!" I cried, as a bone clattered up to me. A bug-eyed Erik Stotz came hopping after it. He scooped up the bone and cried, "See? See?"

Flashlight apps swerved to the spot he was pointing at. It was an enormous crack in the wall, filled to bursting with extremely old objects. Not Picassos this time.

"Bones," I whispered. A massive pile of bones.

"Look!" someone cried. "I think that bone has been chewed on! That's sick!"

I backed far, far away.

"It's probably just coincidence," I muttered. "If there are famous paintings hidden in corridors, why not bones in a crack? It's totally normal."

Yeah. Normal. And those bite marks were obviously left by the rats.

You don't believe in the rats, I reminded myself.

My whole body shivered. I thought about Kayla sneaking off on her own. How could she possibly know what was out there? How sick it was?

I bit my lip as Ms. Wellington squeezed by. For a split-second, I considered ratting on Kayla. What if she got lost in the museum? Or injured?

Then I remembered that Darius and I were planning to sneak away, too, for our movie. Not to mention that Stetler would kill me for blabbing.

Stetler. Ugh.

Why did it have to be Stetler?

My neck itched, so I spun around—and nearly swallowed a cell phone. Darius was shoving it up to my face.

"Dude," I gasped. "Are you…filming me?"

"That's the job." Darius grinned. "Every movie needs B-roll footage. Especially ours, since we're making it up on the fly. But that's in the past, so buck up. Things are about to get wild!"

He pointed ahead. Sunlight was flooding into a vast hall full of gray-and-brown bones. I almost cried out in shock.

"TRIASSIC PARK," said a sign in the archway. "RISE OF THE DINOSAURS."

That's true, I thought. *Dinosaurs first appeared in the Late Triassic Period, which was part of the Mesozoic—*

"C'mon, dude!" said Darius. "Before these bones come alive and attack us!"

"Very funny," I muttered. But I wasn't upset. My chest fizzed with excitement as I squished through the archway and into the widest, brightest, most incredible room I'd ever seen in my life.

Heaven, I thought. *I'm in heaven!*

I let out a whoop as I pushed through the crowd. I couldn't stop staring at the giant exhibits.

Dinosaurs!

Okay, yeah—the real monsters didn't arrive until the Jurassic and Cretaceous periods, which came after. But that didn't mean the Triassic dinosaurs were all shrimps.

I paused in front of a skeleton as big as a truck. And it wasn't even the biggest! There were tiny raptors that stood like ostriches and giant plant-eating brutes, which made me think of how Mrs. Fawcett would look as a dinosaur.

Sunlight streamed through the vertical windows. I sucked down huge gulps of clean and fresh air. There was space for everyone inside the massive exhibit hall. My entire *school* could've fit here—including the building.

"What species is that?" Darius said suddenly.

He pointed to the skeleton rising behind me.

"Please say it's a carnivore, Arlo. I can't have you posing next to a vegetarian. Or can I?" Darius's eyes glimmered. *"In a world* where evil plants have turned dinosaurs into brain-eating zombies…"

His goofy voice trailed away as he warped back to Spielberg planet. But not me. I was still trying to answer the question.

What species is that?

My eyebrows scrunched as I peered at the skeleton.

Not to brag, but I know a lot about dinosaurs. My dad is Dr. Fossil, after all. There are lots of ways to separate the herbivore, a.k.a. plant-eaters, from the carnivores. But mostly you want to focus on one factor.

Teeth.

Herbivores have smaller and flatter teeth than the carnivores. Their teeth are straighter, too, not bent, and there are a whole lot of them.

Carnivores like the *Tyrannosaurus rex* are the opposite. They have these huge chompers that curl like a claw. Their teeth look incredibly dangerous. And they are. They're used to rip into flesh. To munch bone!

I rose on my tiptoes, squinting up at the skull. At its teeth. I kept tilting my head. Changing angles.

What kind of teeth did it have?

Wait.

Where *were* its teeth? Why couldn't I see them?

My skin prickled. I had an eerie feeling all the sudden. Then again, maybe I'd missed something. What if the teeth were too tiny to spot from the ground?

I strained my neck, leaning closer. I stared and stared at the skull. Then I gasped as its bony jaw turned to me.

Turned to me.

"Aaaaaahhhh!" I shrieked. "AAAAAHHHHHHHH!"

19

"DARIUS MORELAND! NO TOUCHING!"

I glanced left and saw Darius leaning over the guard-rail. He slipped his hand off the dinosaur's tail bone.

"Sorry, Ms. Wellington!" he boomed. Then he turned to me. "No offense, Arlo. Couldn't resist."

"Y-You were shaking the skeleton?"

Darius grinned. "Who knew Dr. Arlo Vreeland could scream like that?"

I scowled at him. But not for long. Ms. Wellington was waving the entire class over.

"Sketchpads out, people!" she said with a clap. "Yes, even you, Erik. You're a person!"

"Am not!" Erik squeaked.

Everyone else was groaning and pulling out pencils.

"Now class," said Ms. Wellington, "I want each of you to choose a dinosaur to sketch. Draw the skeleton as accurately as you can, then do a second sketch of what you think your dinosaur actually looked like."

"Like a bird!" someone said.

"No, a lizard!"

"Only bones!" shouted Erik.

"Let's pray the sunlight holds out," Mrs. Fawcett grumbled. "The Ditzy Director forgot to turn on the electricity." She flipped the light switch uselessly. When it didn't work, guess which kids she decided to glare at?

"C'mon," I told Darius. We grabbed our sketchpads and slipped away before Mrs. Fawcett decided to track us.

That's the trouble with class trips. You can't mess around the whole time. There's always somebody watching you.

I took a seat beside a *Plateosaurus* skeleton (I think) and eyed the blank yellow page in my sketchpad. Darius flopped down beside me. His pen was scribbling like crazy. I heard a soft FLUMP! as his sketchpad slammed shut.

"Done!" he announced.

I gaped at him. "Seriously?"

Darius opened his sketchpad and revealed the most pathetic-looking stick figure drawing I'd ever seen in my life.

"Oops! Forgot the second one." He grabbed the pen in my hand, scribbled on his page for two seconds, then closed the sketchpad again. "Man, I love art assignments. Can I draw yours?"

I snatched my pen away. "No!"

"Hurry up, then. This is our chance. While everyone else is stuck drawing, we can sneak off and film. No one will see us."

"Just give me a minute, okay?"

"What's wrong?"

I took a deep breath. "I'm not sure."

I looked up at the *Plateosaurus* skeleton. *Plateosaurus* is probably the most common fossil on Earth. It first appeared in the Triassic Period, and I'd seen sketches of its bone structure hundreds of times. So how come Uncle Leo's *Plateosaurus* looked…wrong? My skin tingled as I examined its tail bone and ribs. I was getting real creepy vibes all the sudden.

FLUMP!

I closed the sketchpad and pulled out Dad's packet of bone diagrams. Darius gave me a sour look.

"Just relax," I said. "I've got to check something."

I found the *Plateosaurus* page right away. I held it up side by side with the skeleton.

"I knew it," I muttered.

The *Plateosaurus* in Dad's packet was different. The drawing had several more ribs, plus this thing called a sternal plate, and at least a dozen more vertebra.

But the missing bones weren't what scared me the most. I flipped through more pages until I found a sketch of the giant, curved teeth that extruded from the skeleton's jaw.

My blood chilled.

Just as I suspected, the teeth didn't belong to the *Plateosaurus* species. They didn't belong to ANY plant-eater. They were carnivore teeth.

Tyrannosaurus rex.

"Hem hem!" said a voice.

I turned and saw Mrs. Fawcett bearing down on me. Her beady eyes gleamed with triumph.

"Caught you red-handed!" she crowed. "You aren't drawing this dinosaur. You're tracing lines from this abominable cheat sheet!"

She grabbed for Dad's packet. I pushed it out of reach, which just made her madder.

"HOW DARE YOU!" Mrs. Fawcett roared.

All the blood drained from my face. I felt like a sack of meat in front of a hungry *T. rex*.

"What's going on here?" Ms. Wellington said, interrupting things.

Saving my life.

I explained about Dad's packet and the project he'd given me. I had to fudge a few details, saying it was the *Plateosaurus* he wanted to catalog, not the *Creeposaurus rex*. But if a lie saves your life, is it really a lie?

"How creative!" said Ms. Wellington. "I approve! Perhaps when we're all finished drawing, we can test our illustrations against your father's bone diagrams."

"Hmph," said Mrs. Fawcett. She was still glaring daggers, looking for new ways to punish me, probably, when a sudden BOOOM! sent her rushing off in another direction.

Yes. Erik Stotz had been climbing a skeleton.

"CRIMINAL MISCHIEF!" Mrs. Fawcett bellowed. "I'LL KILL HIM!"

"Oh dear," said Ms. Wellington. "I'd better go stop her. She might."

HAVE YOU EVER PLAYED Jenga before? It's this game where you start by stacking a bunch of thin wooden blocks into a tower shape. Then the players each take turns pulling blocks out. The point of the game is to remove as many blocks as you can before the tower collapses.

It's a pretty fun game. My family plays it a lot.

But that's not the point.

The point is, I spent the next ten minutes comparing the Triassic Park skeletons to the diagrams in Dad's packet, and the whole time, I couldn't stop thinking about Jenga.

Bones in every exhibit were missing.

Not every bone. Not enough to collapse a whole skeleton. But more than enough to leave the Triassic Park exhibits looking like late-stage Jenga towers. They were teetering on the edge of collapse.

If one more bone was removed, they would drop. I felt sure of it.

It's normal to see incomplete skeletons, I told myself. *Sometimes bones get lost or destroyed, or they're misplaced during the collection phase.*

I nodded silently. I knew all that. But this felt like too many bones. I did some quick calculations using Dad's diagrams.

Want to know how many bones were missing from every exhibit, on average?

Thirty to forty percent.

Yes. I counted the bones of four separate skeletons. Then six skeletons. Then eight. By skeleton number ten, my heart was pounding so hard, it almost crashed through my ribs.

What if I told you *I* was missing thirty to forty percent of my skeleton, too?

Wait. Didn't I already tell you that?

The packet of bone diagrams slipped from my hand. I dropped to one knee, feeling faint. All the energy left my body and I felt like a bottomless pit.

I wanted to cry out in terror.

How could the biggest mystery in my life—my freak, boneless body—be related to a bunch of fossils in Uncle Leo's museum?

And what about the other stuff? Living bones? The wink from Uncle Leo as that *thing* inside of the armor abducted me?

How could it just be coincidence?

What was going on here, exactly?

A low moan slithered out of my throat. All my bones squished together as I knelt on the floor, feeling ice water slurp through my veins.

"This is great stuff," Darius whispered. "The hero in crisis. Keep going!"

I watched his cell phone swing right, toward a short skeleton with long, bird-like talons.

Eoraptor, I thought dizzily. *Three feet tall and three claws.*

So how come I only saw one? A single claw on each foot? Where were the other two?

My bones shook again. There was too much weirdness in this crazy museum. Too many creepy connections.

"What is going on?" I moaned. *"Why is this happening?"*

I stared at the skull, as if the tiny *Eoraptor* could answer me. And that's when I saw it. The missing claws were *right there*. Fused to either side of its jawbone.

They looked exactly like Creep fangs.

The sunlight dimmed suddenly. The air turned a fuzzy gray color as murmurs swept through the hall. I was amazed at how distant they sounded. How far had Darius and I wandered? I suddenly realized we were nowhere near the rest of our class.

I looked around. Storm clouds clung to the windows. There was a sharp CRACK! of thunder as rain buckets pinged off the ceiling.

The last ray of sunlight dissolved.

The exhibit went black.

Oh no, I thought. *Oh-no, oh-no, oh-no.*

As I fumbled for my cell phone, my eyes caught on the *Eoraptor* skull. Only its fanged silhouette was still visible. Cloaked in darkness, it loomed like a bloodthirsty demon.

Then one of its eyes turned bright red.

·20

I HATE THE DARK. Did I say that already?

Fossils are great when you can actually see them. I love inspecting all the tiny ridges and grooves—the swirly shapes that look so strange in bright sunlight, or even under Dad's microscope.

It's like exploring an alien world. And best of all, while you do it, you're safe. There's light everywhere. Nothing is hidden. Any fossil you find has been dead for millions and billions of years, so it can't fill with eerie red light.

It can't move.

The words rang through my head, like a chant, as the *Eoraptor* stared at me. Crimson light burst from its empty eye sockets, making me shiver. I suddenly realized the freaky red light was coming from *inside of its skull.*

Not its eyeballs. Its BRAIN.

Its bone-crunching, carnivore brain.

Panic surged through my chest. "D-Don't eat me!" I gasped, except my voice came out warped and distorted, echoing across the pitch-dark exhibit hall. It was then I started hearing things. Strange murmurs and scrapes.

Dinosaurs, I thought crazily. *More dinosaurs!*

My skin crawled. I felt their dark silhouettes closing in on me.

Hunting me.

Panicked, I suddenly flung out my hands.

"I surrender!" I moaned. "I surrender!"

I held my breath. My shaking hands blocked my view of the *Eoraptor* that wanted to eat me. But I knew it was still there. Still advancing.

But wait. How did the back of my hand turn bright red?

Slowly at first, I waved my hand around. The strange beam didn't follow my hand, but filled the *Eoraptor* skull that my hand had been blocking. I moved my hand back. The eerie red light reappeared on it. I was still squinting, trying to puzzle things out, when the light swerved abruptly. It moved in crazed loops across the exhibit hall, like a lightning bug with a jet engine upgrade.

"What the—?" I muttered.

Looking round, I saw the dark outline of what could only be my teacher, Ms. Wellington. She was swinging her laser light, sweeping it across the pitch-dark exhibit hall.

I followed the zooming red dot until it settled on top of a fossil. For a split-second, a clown face appeared—just as it had in our classroom this morning, when Ms. Wellington aimed her laser at Stetler.

I gasped in relief. *Oh thank God.*

So the *Eoraptor* hadn't come alive after all. I was safe! Or…was I?

I couldn't stop thinking about those eye lights. Hadn't I seen them before? Weren't they the same piercing red color as the *Creeposaurus rex* skull I'd seen in the tower?

There was a sudden BOOM! as the rainfall increased.

"Order!" cried a voice. And then, "Criminal mischief!"

Flashlight apps swept through the darkness like search lights. All but one, at least. Erik Stotz must've bought the premium version of the app because he was wreaking havoc with the multiple options.

"No police lights, Erik!" Mrs. Fawcett bellowed.

"Arggh! Not the strobe effect, either!"

I was still a long way from the group. Even still, Erik's light stung my eyes. Have you ever seen a strobe light before? The flashing light makes the world look like a stop-motion video. You can't help but think the people around you are moving.

Or the skeletons.

A fresh wave of fear flooded into me. Deep down, I knew I was probably safe. But try explaining that to your heart that never stops beating, or your lungs that keep gasping for air.

I'm not the Dalai Lama. I can't calm my nerves with a thought.

My heart thumped against my rib cage, almost as fast as the strobe light.

I have to go, I thought. *I have to get out of here.*

I started walking the other direction.

Then I started to run.

My bones slurped and I didn't care. I swept past dozens of Triassic Park skeletons. Every fossil loomed darker than the next as I distanced myself from the light.

I couldn't stop running.

I had to escape.

Yes, I was totally freaked. I didn't know what was real anymore. Not the skeletons. Not the SLURP! of my knee-caps. Not the sharp CLUNK! of footsteps behind me.

Wait. Footsteps?

I looked around and saw Darius. The whites of his eyes glowed as bright as his cell phone. I made a rude gesture at the camera. But as the seconds ticked by, I calmed down.

Eventually I relaxed enough to let Darius feed me some lines.

"Be on the lookout for *Creeposaurus rex* bones," I said bravely.

"If that *THING* has hurt Dr. Yacob, I'm going to break every bone in its bony body!" I said heroically.

"This *Chindesaurus* skeleton is missing half its caudal vertebra and most of its ribs," I said knowledgeably (but also with rising alarm).

Against the odds, I was really enjoying myself. I started hamming it up. I waved my fists in the air and spoke extra loud for the camera. I knew Darius was still filming me.

Our footsteps echoed across the tile as we moved deeper into what was beginning to feel like an endless ex-hibit—until a sudden noise made me skid to a halt.

Okay, fine. A sudden *absence* of noise. I squinted over my shoulder—it was still pretty dark—and saw the blurred outline of Darius. He was hunched over, filming a spot where the floor met the wall.

I shuffled over.

"Darius?" I whispered. "What's wrong? Did I flub a line?"

As I drew closer, I heard a noise like running water. Like a stream trickling over the rocks.

No. It was more of a clinking sound.

Clinking…rocks?

I felt a strange chill as I settled in next to Darius. An icy wind swirled around us.

"Darius?" I said nervously.

Darius put a finger to his lips. Still holding his phone, he jerked his head at the floor. I grabbed my own phone and shined a light on the spot he was filming.

Guess what I found there?

A river.

A river of bones.

21

DARIUS WAS SHAKING like a leaf. His wide eyes remained fixed on the bones as they shivered and clicked up the wall.

"Bones," he whispered. "Moving bones…"

"I told you they were real," I said.

"No. No." Darius shook his head groggily. "This can't be happening. It must be the rats. A giant family of rats."

"What?" I said. "No!"

"The rats are hiding beneath the bones," said Darius. "Gathering materials…to bring back to their rat queen."

He's losing his mind, I thought.

"You're confusing rats with ants, dingbat! Seriously, how did you make it past kindergarten?"

Darius didn't speak. The only sound was the low clink of bones rushing by.

Living bones. Zombie bones.

At this point, I wish I could lie and say I identified most of them. *Herrerasaurus* claws. *Panphagia* teeth. Any bone from the hilariously-named *Pantydraco* (a real dinosaur).

But I'm not my dad. I can't judge the name and date of a fossil that fast. Nevertheless, even Darius, the bone-stealing rat true believer, pieced a few facts together after a massive, fanged skull went skittering under his kneecap.

"Dino bones!" he gasped. "T-These are bones from the Triassic Park exhibit!"

Well, duh. Of course they were. The question was, where were they going? And did we *really* want to find out?

That's when Darius went full-on insane. His whole face lit up.

"Yes!" he cried out when I asked him. "We have to follow the rats! This is exactly the kind of break we've been waiting for!"

He grabbed my shoulders. I couldn't believe how fast his mood shifted. He was back on planet Spielberg again. I could tell by the glittering light in his eyes.

"Don't you see, Arlo? This is how *Creeposaurus rex* disappeared from the Entrance Hall. The rats took the bones! They didn't eat them. They carried them back to their secret underground rat hill!"

"Secret underground rat hill?" I echoed. "You mean like an *ant* hill?"

Darius completely whiffed on my sarcasm.

"If we find the missing Creep bones, we'll be heroes," he said excitedly. "Celebrities! Our movie will get *millions* of views." He exhaled a breath. "This is incredible. The rats are the secret villains of the story. What a twist! No one will see it coming!"

I cleared my throat roughly.

"A family of rats couldn't pilot a suit of armor," I pointed out. "They can't make a *Creeposaurus rex* stick its head out a castle window. Also, how do you explain the red eyes?"

"Mutant rats," Darius insisted. "Mutant rats who are hiding a dark secret in the icy depths of their rat hill!"

He leapt to his feet with a laugh. I suddenly felt his palms on my back, pushing me toward the gushing bone river.

"Move it, Arlo! You have to follow them!"

I coughed. "Excuse me? *I* have to follow them? *Me?*"

"Yes, you! You're Dr. Arlo Vreeland, the fearless hero. I'm just the dude with the camera."

I opened my mouth to complain and then stopped. Like I said before, it's no use trying to argue with Darius. He always wins because he never listens. Especially when he's directing a movie.

So yes, with no better option, I pushed forward, leading the way as we tracked the bone river. I kept my flashlight app aimed at my feet. Every step brought more freezing air into my lungs. My hands were trembling and my breath came out in bursts of thick fog. Not to mention those clinking, chittering bones made my heart fill with dread.

What awful power was making them move like this? And why was it bitter cold? Where were we heading, the North Pole?

I was totally freaking out. "What about school?" I said. "We could get in serious trouble for ditching."

"The blackout is a perfect excuse," said Darius. "It's too dark to find our way back. And since we didn't *mean* to get lost—not at first, anyway—it isn't really a lie."

"You think?"

Darius shrugged. "If they don't believe us, we'll just say we went looking for Stetler and Dr. Yacob. I mean, Kayla."

My breath quickened. *Kayla!*

How could I forget about Kayla? *Of course* Kayla was still out there, wandering the halls of a pitch-dark museum. Yes, she'd warned me not to chase after her, or whatever. But that was before I'd found proof that some of these bones were alive. Kayla might be brave—even braver than Dr. Hannah Yacob in the movie—but no way could she handle a river of bones.

Neither can you, I thought randomly.

I inhaled a breath, sweeping my eyes across the bones that flowed on and on, heading God knows where, through the shivering darkness.

I felt an inexplicable thrill in my chest.

"Dr. Arlo Vreeland can handle it," I whispered.

"Say what now?" said Darius.

I puffed out my chest, grinning over my shoulder. My voice came out perfectly calm and a full octave deeper.

"I said, all right. No more excuses. Let's do this!"

I clapped my hands and stepped forward—not as Arlo the Freak, but as Arlo, actual crazy person, alias Dr. Arlo Vreeland, a man of vast talent and bottomless self-belief, tasked with a mission worth risking my life for.

"Kayla," I whispered. "I'm coming."

22

MY NEW SELF-BELIEF lasted all of three seconds. Then Darius kicked a dinosaur bone at my leg. I felt a sharp chill as it slid down my thigh and started coiling around my legs, like a boa constrictor.

At least that's the image I had in my head.

"Aaaaahhhh!" I shrieked. "AAAAAHHHH!"

Darius's booming laughter rang all through the corridor where we'd followed the bones into.

What can I say? It's not easy being a hero. And honestly, Kayla isn't exactly a damsel in distress. She's not that big, but she's clever and quick. She could probably take ME in a fight, one on one.

And Stetler could kill you, I reminded myself.

My bones slurped at the thought. I gripped the stone wall for balance, almost collapsing right then.

What on Earth was I doing? I wasn't a hero, and this wasn't some Hollywood movie. There were real bones in that river. Living bones. And what was my plan if I *really* found Kayla? I could barely take care of MYSELF.

My heart raced and my breathing came out in short gasps. It was a few seconds before I finally talked myself back into character. What can I say? Anxiety is tough. It chews at your heart, like a rat.

Sorry. Ugh. Bad example!

It was around then that Darius came trotting up to me.

"Cut!" he yelled. "Cut!"

He snaked his arm around my shoulder, and I prepared myself for some kind of super lame pep talk. Director to actor.

"Look, Arlo," he began, "I know you're probably worried about your goofy hair breaking the illusion that you're really a hero—"

I blinked my eyes. *"What?"*

"—so I brought you a little something." Darius rummaged around in his bookbag. "Changing wardrobe this late into filming is hardly ideal, but in this case, I think the benefits outweigh the costs. Ah, found it!"

A couple Cine-Blocks came flying out the zipper pocket, followed by a flimsy, sombrero-like object.

"A…cowboy hat?" I said.

"It's supposed to be Indiana Jones," said Darius.

He held it out to me.

I took the hat and rolled it through my fingers. "This is plastic," I said. "Darius, is this a party favor? There's *glitter.*"

"We're on a budget, okay? Try it on."

He pressed the hat onto my head, tightening the belt so it wouldn't fall off.

"Looking good, Dr. V!" he exclaimed. "Do you feel good?"

I didn't trust Darius's opinion *at all*, so I put my phone into selfie mode and held it out like a mirror.

Hey, I thought. *This isn't half bad.*

I made a grim face. Then a sullen face. Then my lips formed a smirk as I winked at the camera.

"You're welcome," Darius laughed as he backpedaled into filming position.

We walked for a couple more minutes. The bones were clicking louder than ever. The river seemed to grow *wider* at times, which was strange. Nevertheless, I felt surprisingly decent. I spoke my lines clearly and well. As a matter of fact, I felt braver.

Here's a secret I've learned: sometimes clothes are like magic. I'm talking about costumes and masks. Even cheap plastic hats. Because when your clothes change, it tricks your brain into thinking all kinds of *other* things about you change, too. I don't know why our brains work this way. They just do.

So no wonder superheroes wear pink suits and full-body onesies. It's less about protecting their secret identities than shifting perspectives. Making THEM believe they can save the city. Defeat the archvillain. Rescue the girl of their dreams from a zombie queen's lair. Ahem. Rescue their ex-best friend who's a girl. But with long silver hair. Perfect cheekbones…

"Arlo! Hey! Look at this!"

Darius was eyeing the corridor wall.

"Let me guess," I said. "Another Picasso?"

Then I focused my vision.

Not a Picasso. Not even a Vincent Van Gogh.

It was another huge crack in the wall. The bone river emitted a frenzy of clicking, creaking, scraping noises as it surged through the three-foot-wide gap in the stone, disappearing into the slithery darkness beyond.

A blast of freezing wind swept through the crack.

"So...cold..." I said, trembling.

"There's some sort of *slime* in there," said Darius. "It's oozing out the crack. See? What *is* that?"

I leaned closer. I knew what it was, all right. It was the same freaky sludge left behind by the bone that attacked me. The one from inside the zombie suit of armor. The one Kayla and Stetler had secretly tracked down a different dark corridor...

"There's bits of slime in the river, too," said Darius, bending over the bones. "It must work like grease. It stops the bones from clumping together. Keeps them moving, you know?"

I shined my cell phone light into the crack. There was some sort of *tunnel* inside. Swirling shapes jutted out of the walls. They looked a lot like the walls outside the museum—all these eerie, bright colors—except the tunnel patterns were thicker and wilder. I craned forward. More than anything, it looked like a cave full of fossils. The kind of thing paleontologists block off with ropes and try to excavate.

A dig site.

My brain gave a sudden jolt. How did I know that? Okay, sure, I had vague memories of Dad bringing me out on his fossil digs. We'd strap in and hop in his truck. I was super young. Five years old maybe? Eventually Mom made him stop taking me after I tripped in a hole. But I barely remembered it.

Until now, I thought.

The sudden connection made my nerves tingle. That's why I really freaked out when I saw what Darius did with his foot.

He was dipping his shoe in the bone river. Then his other shoe.

"DON'T TOUCH IT!" I cried. "BACK AWAY!"

"They're just rats, dude," said Darius. "Rats are super strong, right? They can carry up to fifty times their body weight." He grinned at me, as if he'd just won first prize at the Science Fair.

"Wrong!" I shot back. "Those are ants! ANTS do that—"

Darius wasn't listening. "I want to see if they'll support my body weight," he said. "What if we could ride the rats into the tunnel? It could work like a tracking shot. Imagine the footage we'd get!"

I stared at Darius.

My best friend was an alien. A certified alien.

Let me stop the story right now and tell you some facts about Darius.

He's a wimp.

He's not brave. He's not reckless. Despite his size (which isn't much smaller than Stetler) he's actually more of a coward than I am. He never stands up for himself. He always, always backs away from a fight.

But here's something else: he goes *completely insane* for his movies. He'll do whatever it takes for a shot. It alters his whole personality. Talk about wearing a costume. For Darius, directing a live-action movie is like wearing a cutting-edge Iron Man suit.

It makes him feel indestructible.

Even when he definitely, definitely isn't!

"Darius, stop!" I cried. "Back away!"

"No worries, Arlo. I've got this."

"You don't! Those bones aren't what you think. They're alive! They can wriggle and clump together and even grab hold of your—"

"WAAAAAAHHHHHHHHH!" cried a voice.

There was a violent CRUNCH! as the river seized Darius by the ankles and started dragging him down. I watched as bones slithered onto his legs. Up his waist. Up his bookbag! The hand holding his cell phone fell limp at his side.

My jaw clenched.

Stiff with fear, I watched the tiny cell phone light bob through the bones as they flowed through the crack and into the tunnel beyond, taking Darius with them. His muffled screams echoed over the darkness.

"AAARRRRRRLLLLOOOOO!"

23

I DON'T KNOW HOW LONG I stood there. Heart shaking, I stared down the tunnel. Eventually my flashlight app timer ran out and the world went pitch-dark. Chittering, screeching sounds rose from the bones, but I couldn't see anything.

You want to talk about fear?

Imagine being trapped in a maze-like museum with no light and a river of zombie bones rushing past you—a river that could spread to your feet any second. Because how would you know? You could try to run, but if you made one false step...if you brushed the edge of a bone with your toe...or even a loose shoestring...

Just imagine that for a second.

Then imagine being Darius Moreland. I could still hear his cries rising out of the tunnel.

"Aaaarrrrlllllooo...Heeeellllppppp meeeee!"

But what could I do? How could I possibly save him?

What if I told you that, looking back, this was the pivotal moment? A lot of crazy stuff was about to happen to me because of the decision I made right this second.

But it didn't need to.

I could've turned back. I could've escaped down the corridor, found the rest of my class and survived. Probably.

So how come I aimed my flashlight app into the crack?

How come I stepped closer to the rushing bone river?

Because I was just as crazy as Darius. I couldn't think straight. I was too caught up in playing Dr. Arlo Vreeland, trying to impersonate a hero and future Academy Award winner.

I adjusted my hat and switched my phone into selfie mode. I eyed the screen with a Hollywood scowl.

"Dr. Arlo Vreeland reporting. As of this moment, the last of my colleagues has vanished. I am the sole survivor, trapped in a foreign land, surrounded on all sides by unknown assailants."

I spun the camera to face the tunnel wall.

"These are the rare fossils we've been searching for. Fossils worth millions of dollars. If I stay here, I could chisel them out. But I won't. I'm going after my friends."

I swallowed hard.

"This will not be my final report. I will not cower. I will not fail. See you at base camp. Dr. Arlo Vreeland, signing off."

I closed the camera app and boldly stepped forward. I didn't give myself even one breath to reconsider. I moved instantly.

There was a CRUNCH! as my heel touched the river. I immediately felt bones creeping over my shins. An icy chill stopped my heart. I sank deeper. It felt like doing a pencil-dive into a giant Slurpee. But I persevered. At least until the bones reached my neck.

"Gah!" I shrieked.

That's when reality exploded my movie scene. My chest spasmed. I started shaking and gasping, fighting the pull of the river.

But too late.

The living bones sent me speeding toward the wall. The crack loomed impossibly wide, like a mouth. Like the jaws of some skeletal whale that was breathing me into its belly.

That was the last thought I had.

Then the darkness consumed me.

24

COLD. I WAS COLD! Freezing bones clunked off my arms and legs. They slid around in the slip-'n'-slide sludge that connected them. My lungs heaved. I couldn't stop gasping. My lips were wet with slime, blue with cold, and pinched from extreme lack of oxygen. The only thing missing was a pipe leading up to a charter bus bathroom.

Ugh. That *still* isn't funny.

I blinked the sludge from my eyes. Was this how dinosaurs felt, getting trapped in the tar pits?

Stay focused, I thought. *You can find Darius. At least try. What do you have to lose?*

"My life," I whined. "My body temperature. The rest of my bones."

Stop moaning and do something! cried the voice in my head.

I felt a rush of adrenaline. Dr. Arlo Vreeland, was that you? I started flailing my arms, trying to wriggle free. I was shocked to find the weight of the bones disappearing. I swam forward, driving my arms and legs like a fish.

(A fish with four limbs? I don't know).

Wherever I went, the living bones slid away. Their icy grip couldn't hold me. I was slippery like an eel. All skin and no skeleton.

Suddenly I was swimming downriver. Escaping!

My swim was so easy, it almost felt like the bones were afraid of me. They gripped my legs and very quickly let go, leaving huge swaths of sludge in their wake.

A wild thought crossed my mind.

Did they know about my missing bones? Could they tell I'd been picked clean already? My skeleton was teetering on the brink of collapse, like the *Plateosaurus* from the Triassic Park exhibit. Maybe the river had a rule about breaking things. Maybe it just loved winning Jenga.

I could find out the truth, I thought crazily. *If I keep swimming, if I follow the bones to the end of the tunnel…they won't hurt me…probably…*

My thoughts were interrupted by an echoing shriek.

"AAAAAaaaahhhhhh!" it cried.

("AAAaahhhhh!")

("Aaaahhh!")

("Aah!")

My heart jolted. *Darius!*

I immediately started kicking my legs. Speeding up. I broke into a furious freestyle. You wouldn't *believe* how fast I was. I know I didn't. My flopping arms and legs worked like fins.

How had I never tried swimming before?

I could be the next Michael Phelps, I thought.

I poked my head above the sludge-line. Where was Darius? I tried to peer through the darkness. But I'm not a cat. I couldn't see squat. So I turned my head sideways and listened.

I heard the SLAP! of arms thrashing around. The CLINK! of Cine-Blocks crammed in a bookbag. I rushed toward the source of the noise: a big, frizzy ball. I clamped my hands on it.

"Got you!"

"AAAHHHHH!" Darius shrieked. Then he coughed up some sludge and said, "Arrrrloo?"

I released his hair and swam beside him, flashing a big, goofy grin. Which was pretty dumb. Darius couldn't see in the dark, either.

But wait. How come I could see him?

Not much of him. But more and more every second.

"Hang on!" I told Darius.

I grabbed his bookbag and started swimming him sideways. There was a flicker of light up ahead. Not the end of the river.

Another wall crack.

But why was light streaming out? Shouldn't the crack have been dark, like the rest of the museum?

There was no time to think. As the river rolled forward, I looped my legs around Darius's bookbag straps. I waited for the crack to rise into view. Then, at just the right moment, I leapt up and dove for it.

I flew like a dolphin. A flying fish!

Light stung my eyes as I burst through the gap. My stomach skidded onto solid stone ground. I spread my arms out to avoid being swept back inside.

"Darius!" I yelled. "Are you still with me? Climb up!"

"Unnnngghhh," Darius moaned.

He pinched my leg like a lobster. I could feel the bone river pounding his body, trying to sweep him away. And okay, I felt some other things, too—like the squishes and slurps of my kneecaps.

"Ohh sick! It's like trying to climb a wet noodle!"

"DON'T LET GO!" I cried.

I peered over my shoulder—my neck stretched like a hose—and saw the dark silhouette of a bone rising over the river.

A massive bone. The sternal plate of a *Plateosaurus!*

Huh, I thought. *What are the odds?*

And then—

"DARIUSSS!" I shouted. "LOOOK OUUUTT!"

I shut my eyes, gripping both ends of the wall like a grappling hook, as the sternal plate rushed at Darius. He couldn't dodge while still holding my leg. He had nowhere to hide.

There was a loud CLUNK! from the tunnel, and a deafening "YEEEOOOOWWW!"

A second later, Darius crashed down beside me. The sternal plate had knocked him straight through the crack. He lay there coughing and gagging, wiping slime from his lips.

We'd survived.

Against the odds, we'd fought our way through the zombie bone river and emerged triumphant. Victorious! We were finally back on solid ground in one of the museum's weird, maze-like corridors.

And we weren't alone.

25

THE FIRST CLUE WE WEREN'T by ourselves was the torches. A pair of thin yellow flames danced on the wall, casting shadows and light on our faces.

I peered around.

Originally, I'd assumed we'd landed in one of the corridors. And maybe we had. Only this was the very end of a corridor.

A dead end.

A dusty stone wall stood before us. Darius sprawled beneath the flames, letting his eyelids drift shut as he basked in the heat.

"Careful," I said. "We're not alone. Torches don't light by themselves."

"Electric torches," Darius murmured.

He sounded half-asleep. He was totally out of it. I decided there was no point explaining the electricity was off, meaning these torches had probably been lit by a person.

Or a creature, I thought queasily.

I suddenly heard movement in the corridor.

"Did you hear that?" I hissed at Darius.

"Hear what?" He choked and sat up.

I pointed down the corridor. As I did, even more noises rose from the right, near the wall crack.

I felt a chill down my neck. I suddenly realized how creepy it was, using torches. Forget about who lit them. Using torches means you're basically trapped in the small circle where your light reaches. Everything beyond the circle is black. As in pitch-black.

Not to mention the bone river was clicking like crazy. Plus the corridor noises.

I was really freaked out. I thought about grabbing the torch off the wall—making a run for it—but then Darius spoke.

"So you fell in the river, too?" he said. "Wow, pretty clumsy."

"I didn't fall in," I snapped. "I went on purpose. I saved you!"

Darius shrugged. I could tell his fear was wearing off. He raised his cell phone, which was like Captain America raising his shield, and asked me to repeat my last line for the movie. I don't know if he was serious or just trying to distract himself. I didn't have any better ideas, though, so I did as he asked.

"Amazing you've still got the hat," said Darius. "You should thank the guy who belted it onto your head like a vice."

I rolled my eyes. As Darius filmed, I climbed to my feet, inspecting the wall with the torches. At first I was just hamming it up for the movie. But it turned out the wall was pretty interesting. It wasn't plain like the corridor walls. The stone was older and thicker. Cobwebs clung to the slabs, and dust clung to the cobwebs, and—

"Hey, look at this!" I said. "Someone's *definitely* been here. See? They dusted this off."

I pointed to a clean stretch of wall, without cobwebs or smudges. Something was etched in the stone. All these strange symbols. Pictograms.

I ran my finger across the ridges.

"I wonder what they're saying," I muttered.

"Here Lies The Sorcerer's Tomb," Darius translated.

My heart froze. "What the—? How did you—?"

Darius cackled. He pointed to a line clearly written in English.

HERE LIES THE SORCERER'S TOMB
ONLY THE PANICKED SHALL PASS

"Wow," I breathed. "This is incredible."

My eyes flicked from the English to the pictograms and back. I found at least two distinct types of pictogram, each roughly the same size and shape as the English.

"I think this might be a Rosetta Stone situation," I said.

"Duolingo!" said Darius. "I've got the app on my phone."

"No, doofus. Not the language app! The Rosetta Stone is this ancient stone tablet—"

"—with the same writing in three different scripts," Darius interjected. "Ancient Egyptian Demotic, Ancient

Egyptian Hieroglyphic, and Ancient Greek. It's famous because it helped researchers decipher the Ancient Egyptian language, since we already knew Ancient Greek."

My jaw dropped as I stared at him.

"What?" said Darius. "I saw it in an Ancient Egypt documentary once. I was looking for *The Mummy Returns.*"

I eyed the Tomb with mounting excitement. Did Uncle Leo even know it was down here? Duh, of course he did. The Sorcerer's Tomb was clearly marked on the sign in the Entrance Hall. Who else could've written it?

The better question was, had anyone explored the Tomb yet?

We could be looking at a real discovery here. Just as cool as the missing *Creeposaurus rex* skeleton. (More on that later).

I jogged down the wall, sweeping my hands through the dust. Were there more carvings to discover? More secrets?

Yes!

A quick search revealed two separate panels, one clean, and one caked in cobwebs. A tall archway rose in between.

"An entrance!" I said excitedly. "A door to the Tomb!"

Since the door was sealed shut, Darius and I focused on the panels.

"HEART GATE," said the first. "Lend your heart."

"BONE GATE," said the second. "Lend your bones."

The Bone Gate was empty, but the slot beneath the Heart Gate glowed an eerie red color. Something solid was wedged deep inside.

"Rubies?" said Darius. "Ms. Wellington's laser light?"

Eyes, I thought crazily. The Heart Gate glowed the same freaky red as the *Creeposaurus rex* I'd spotted outside.

My thoughts raced. Could the Sorcerer's Tomb and that giant, fanged skull be connected? Were red eyes the mark of a zombie? A bone zombie?

"Arlo, chill," said Darius. "You're totally freaking out."

"Sorry," I muttered. "It's just that, well—"

I paused, wondering whether to try explaining again.

"No, I get it," said Darius. "Bone Gate. Lend your bones. Kind of hits a nerve for you, doesn't it?"

It did, actually, now that he mentioned it.

I eyed the Bone Gate again. The slot beneath the panel was empty. Unfilled.

"So unfair," Darius sighed. "They should let us in already. You're, like, the biggest bone lender in history, right? How many bones are you missing? A thousand?"

"A human skeleton has two hundred and six bones," I recited. But on the inside, my heart trembled. Something in Darius's speech made me wince.

The biggest bone lender in history. *In history.*

Me.

I got a real creepy vibe all the sudden. It was the same prickly feeling I'd felt in the tunnel, like this weird déjà vu.

Had I already been here before? Ridiculous, I know.

But you can't fight a feeling.

I suddenly spun on my heel. I could've sworn I heard movement behind me. More footsteps.

It's just the river, I told myself.

But I couldn't take my eyes off the darkness. I knew something was out there. I felt it.

Darius was still inspecting the Tomb. "It's a puzzle," he said. "Each gate needs a specific object. Like a key. I bet you need both keys to open the archway. Since the Heart Gate is already filled by this red junk, we just need a key to the…to the…yo, Arlo! You with me, dude?"

I didn't speak. I didn't dare say a word.

"C'mon, man. I need your help with this—*Oh my God!*"

Darius froze. He'd finally followed my gaze up the corridor.

Eyes. There were piercing red eyes. More than two.

The eye lights advanced with loud slurps and hisses. Bones clinked in the shadows. I uttered a silent prayer to the Hollywood gods.

Make them stop, I begged. *Let the torches form a protective barrier. Don't let them enter the warmth and the light!*

More and more eyes appeared.

Beady eyes. Hungry eyes.

I uttered a wail as the first creature entered the torchlight. It didn't stop or slow down. It plowed forward on claw-ended feet. Fangs like huge fishhooks jutted out of its skull, dribbling with slime from the river.

But for all our panic, and all the freaky red light bursting out, it looked more like blood.

26

"C-CREEP!" DARIUS GASPED. "It's a Creep! Baby Creep!"

"Yeah," I gulped. "A whole litter."

The first skeleton was the smallest. Barely two feet off the ground, it squelched forward on rickety feet.

"Looks really unstable," I whispered.

"At least they're babies," said Darius. "How big are they? Twenty, thirty pounds? Go on, Arlo. You can take 'em!"

Fluffkins is small, I thought. *I can't even take Fluffkins.*

Then my eyes narrowed.

"Hang on. *Me?* Why do *I* have to—HEY!"

There was a mad scramble as Darius ducked behind me before I could duck behind HIM. His bookbag snagged on my hip, making the Cine-Blocks inside shake like crazy.

Guess who noticed?

"Kwweeek?" chirped a Creep.

"Kweeek?"

"Kweeek! Kweeek!"

All seven sets of eyes fixed on ME. Stupid Darius. His bookbag was like a stinking Creep attractor!

"Save me," Darius squeaked.

"Coward," I spat. Then I heard the soft click! of Darius unlocking his camera app. Filming me.

"Double coward!"

More skeletons entered the light. Three feet tall. Four feet tall. The same fiery red color burst from their eye holes. They looked like jack-o'-lanterns on Halloween night. Except those grayish-brown bones wouldn't disintegrate the moment they hit us...

One of the creatures, a sort of *Eoraptor* hybrid, dragged its super-sized claw on the floor, emitting a horrible scritching noise as it crossed beneath the first torch. Its bony snout sniffed the air. Then it turned to me.

Glared at me.

Face trembling, I got my first close-up look at a Creep.

Yes, it was a dinosaur skeleton. Sort of. I knew at once that I wouldn't find its bone diagram in Dad's packet.

The armored plates on its spine tipped me off.

So did the extra two arms.

As best I could tell, the bones came from everywhere. Triassic, Jurassic, Cretaceous. The whole Mesozoic Era. Not just the armored plates, but the super-sized claw, the funny lump on the end of its tail, like an *Ankylosaurus*. The fangs in its skull looked the same as the modified *Eoraptor* from Triassic Park. They were just regular claws jutting out.

Up close, they looked pretty odd. Almost dumb.

But I knew those dumb-looking claws were still more than enough to rip our throats out.

"I can't watch," Darius squealed. He closed his eyes, but not his camera app, as he rolled onto his stomach. His fat bookbag shook like maracas.

Stupid Cine-Blocks, I thought angrily.

Then my eyes widened. Of course!

I suddenly realized what all these creatures reminded me of.

About a year ago, back when Darius and I became friends, one of the first things we did was combine our Cine-Blocks collections. We both owned a ton of cool kits. But kits are boring once you've finished them, so we dismantled our models and spilled all our blocks in this super huge pile. *The Boneyard,* we called it (although it was really just Darius's closet).

We spent hours messing around in there, building these strange, photorealistic creatures and trying to film them as miniatures. No instruction manuals. Just a mandate: build the craziest, wildest, freakiest thing you can think of.

I stared around at the ragtag group of skeletons tracking us. The fangs. The weird spikes. The extra arms and the ball-ended tails. All the coolest parts of a dinosaur skeleton, mixed together.

It had to mean something, right?

CRUNCH!

The not-*Eoraptor* stalked forward—then, out of nowhere, it collapsed! I watched in amazement as its rickety bones burst apart, forming a big, slimy pile that wriggled and slopped, like a bucket of fish.

"What's happening?" Darius squeaked.

"Cross your fingers," I whispered, as more creatures dropped to the ground, melting back into bones.

I had no idea what was happening. But it was good, right? The Creeps were disappearing. I dragged Darius onto his feet, ready to make a run for it (or a brisk walk, or however fast my loose bones could scoot) when one of the bone piles suddenly poked up its head.

Its *huge* head.

The pile surged to its massive, clawed feet. Blazing red eyes towered over us. How tall was it? Six feet? Seven feet? Bones from the other six piles were leaping into place along the skeleton's chest, tail and spine as it stretched even more.

"Nnnoooooo!" I moaned. "T-They're joining forces! Combining!"

"KWEEK! KWEEK!" chirped the half-finished Creep.

What did it want? What was it saying? I didn't know. Didn't care. We had to get out of here. *Now.*

And yeah, I know what you're thinking. The Sorcerer's Tomb. Now would be a perfect time to slot something into the Bone Gate and trigger the door.

But what could we put there?

A bone? One of those sick zombie bones?

Sorry if I didn't want to wrestle an eight-foot-tall Godzilla Creep, trying to snag a loose bone that may or may not even open the Tomb. If the plan failed, I'd be ripped to shreds faster than you can say, 'KWEEK.'

Also, I didn't think of it. I'm not an A+ student like Kayla Caine. With so much panic swirling inside me, the absolute best I could do was summon the spirit of Dr. Arlo Vreeland one more time.

Hopefully not for the last time. But you only live once.

"Stay close to me," I told Darius. "And don't fall behind. This is it. We're attacking."

"W-Wha—?" Darius choked in alarm.

"The bones are shaky," I said. "They'll fly apart if we hit them."

I hope, I thought privately.

"Y-You're crazy, Arlo!"

"That's Dr. Arlo to you," I said, hooking my arm through his bookbag straps. "We go on three. One—two—"

"AAAAHHHHHHH!" shouted Darius.

"AAAAHHHHHHH!" shouted me.

We lurched forward on shivering feet. Our pace was slow. Our steps were uneven. But we couldn't stop now.

The Creep stared us down. Armored plates on its tail and back gleamed in the torchlight. A massive spike jutted out of its chin, beneath slobbery fangs.

My eyes shrank to slits as we ran at it.

"AAAAHHHHHHH!" I cried again.

"OH-GOD-OH-GOD-OH-GOD!" chanted Darius.

Moments from impact, I saw what looked like a streak of white lightning. There was an earsplitting CRUNCH! as the Creep staggered sideways. The lightning kept coming.

CRUNCH! CRUNCH! CRUNCH!

It was over in seconds. I stared at the pile of cracked, ruined bones on the floor.

Had we done that? Had we really just——?

No. A boy's whooping cry filled the air.

"STETLER SMASH!"

My eyelids flew open. Stetler's bald head bounced into view. He danced above the ruined Creep, his huge fists shadow-boxing the empty air.

A few feet behind him stood Kayla. My breath caught in a gasp. She looked incredible. Like a real-life Tomb Raider. Her silver hair waved in the torchlight, like a bone-colored fleece. The smudges on her face and sleeves only made her look tougher.

"Dr. Yacob!" I blurted out. "I mean, Kayla! You're safe now. We – we found you!"

A loose cobweb shook from Kayla's dark eyebrows as she knitted them up in a grin.

No. A scowl.

"ARLO!" she bellowed. "YOU…IDIOT!"

27

KAYLA STALKED OVER, a vein in her neck pulsing angrily.

"I *told you* not to roam the museum! I TOLD YOU!"

"I-I'm sorry!" I said. "I thought you were in trouble. This museum is dangerous. The…the bones are alive!"

Kayla scowled and turned away from me. A second later, however, she came roaring back. Her left arm shot out. I felt a rush of wind as she tore the cowboy hat off my head and almost flung it away.

But she stopped herself.

A smile curled on her lips. She placed the hat on her head, tilting the brim slightly left, so her silver hair swelled beneath it.

Perfect fit.

Darius and I gaped at each other. The plastic brim didn't look so cheap anymore. It looked dashing and brave. Like the hat of a hero.

"Craig, keep them off me," said Kayla. "I need space."

Stetler's shark-like eyes narrowed. "You got it, K."

He shoved me onto the floor next to Darius, who had dropped down pre-emptively, his hands raised in surrender.

"Be a good freak and don't move," Stetler warned.

Then, unzipping his bookbag, he pulled out all kinds of things. A compass. A length of brown rope. A box of party Sparklers with the wrapping torn off...

"*You* lit the torches," I blurted out.

Stetler grinned. "I came prepared. A *real* bookbag isn't just books. It's got all the essentials."

"Respect," said Darius.

Stetler glared at him.

"Okay, okay. Shutting up."

An uneasy silence filled the corridor. The smell of slime mixed with Pearberry body spray as Kayla inspected every inch of the Tomb, sweeping dust off the stone with spread fingers.

"I've been looking for ways to unseal it," she announced. "Craig and I found the first gate already. Then we backtracked up the corridor, looking for more of them. For the life of me, I can't remember how we ever opened the Tomb in the—WHAT IS THAT!"

Kayla's eyes fixed on the empty Bone Gate. She started furiously sweeping it clear, even though it was *already* clear, thanks to me.

"I don't believe it...the second gate was here all along!" She shot a fierce look at Stetler. "You said you checked this part of the wall, Craig!"

Stetler's eyes shrank to pinpoints. "I, uh, meant to inspect it. But there were cobwebs and, uh...I really hate spiders." His huge body trembled.

Darius and I snickered.

"Quiet!" said Stetler. He pinched my arm like a stress toy.

Kayla shook her head at him. "Craig, stop. You don't have to hurt him. Why don't you take your anger out on something a bit more…deserving?"

Kayla nodded at the bones on the floor, then to the empty slot beneath the Bone Gate.

"Lend your bones," she murmured. "Using the Sorcerer's bones seems too easy, but it can't hurt to try."

"Huh?" I said. "The Sorcerer's bones?"

Kayla ignored me. "Can you please fetch me a bone?" she asked Stetler.

Stetler stared across the floor. The loose bones were shaking and flopping. He trembled again.

"I don't mind smashing their skeletons," he mumbled. "But those tiny bones are too creepy. Look at them *wriggling.*" He paused, glaring at me. "Don't say a word, Freak."

I didn't. I was just as creeped out as Stetler.

After a long look, Stetler closed his eyes and jabbed his toe out. A bone soared through the air like a rocket. There was a CLUNK! as it struck the Tomb wall and fell limp.

"Sorry," said Stetler. "Too strong."

I didn't know which was weirder: this whole situation, or the sound of Stetler apologizing.

Kayla had a big smirk on her face. She knelt down and grabbed the bone. I saw her face tighten as the bitter coldness spiked up her arm, but she didn't gasp or cry out. She gritted her teeth, then turned to the Tomb and jammed the bone in the slot.

We all held our breath.

28

NOTHING MOVED. NOTHING SHOOK.

Nothing happened.

After a few empty seconds, the bone wriggled out of the slot and hit the floor again. This time Stetler was ready. He flashed a leg out (even with his eyes closed) and stomped.

There was a sickening CRUNCH!

"That felt good," Stetler growled.

I glanced at Darius. Guess what glowed in his hand?

Yes. A cell phone.

Kayla's eyes swept the Tomb, looking stumped. "Bone Gate…Bone Gate…" she murmured. "Why isn't it open? Why won't it accept me?"

I couldn't hold myself back anymore.

"Why do you care?" I blurted out. "What's so important about the Sorcerer's Tomb? And how come I feel like you knew all this weird stuff would happen today? Like you expected it?"

I took a deep breath.

"Why are you HERE?" I summed up, jabbing my hand at the Tomb.

And why with Stetler? I didn't add.

Kayla ran a thumb through her silvery hair. Her frown deepened. She wouldn't meet my eyes all the sudden.

"I…made a mistake," she said quietly. "I thought I'd fixed it before. I was wrong. He came back."

I stared at her.

"But I can still make things right," she said. "I know I can. I have to. I just need to open—this—gate!"

With a wild cry, Kayla spun round and pounded her fists on the Tomb. The vein in her neck thudded crazily.

"I gave you your stupid bone!" she roared. "How many bones do you want? Take my arm! Take the bones in it! That's what you like, isn't it? ISN'T IT?"

There was a second cry, even wilder, as Kayla shoved *her entire left arm* into the Bone Gate slot. She kept grunting and growling, trying to force her arm deeper into the wall.

"Kayla, stop!" I cried. "You'll hurt yourself!"

"I—don't—care!" she shrieked. "Take my arm, you stupid tomb! Stupid Sorcerer!"

I'd never seen Kayla act this crazy before. She was always so quiet. Especially this year in middle school.

The transformation was shocking.

Nevertheless, as I watched Kayla fighting the Tomb, something clicked in my brain. Suddenly the answer came rushing out of me.

"I know!" I said. "I know what it wants! Put your arm away, Kayla. Try this."

Kayla stopped grunting and blinked at me. I'd already pulled out Uncle Leo's bone invitation. I held it out to her.

Yes.

See, I'm only dumb when *I'm* the one panicking. When my life's not in imminent danger (and okay, when I'm a little bit jealous) I can use my big brain.

At least I hope it's big. Life should be fair, after all.

I saw Kayla's eyes glimmer. I expected her to come rushing in for a hug. *Ohmygosh, Arlo! Where did you find this? It's perfect! You totally saved me! Mwah! Mwah!*

Instead of that, Kayla slapped her own forehead.

"Of course!" she cried—and she rushed up to Stetler. *To Stetler.* She lunged for his bookbag, poked around in it, and pulled out what looked like this weird-looking mirror.

Haha, no. Not a mirror. Another bone invitation.

Her own.

My brain blurred with all the muddled thoughts inside.

"You…got one too?" I gasped. "Why? How? Did Uncle Leo drop it off on your porch this morning?"

Kayla turned the bone in her hands. "Your uncle didn't send these," she replied. "*He* did."

She tapped the Sorcerer's Tomb. When I still looked confused, she showed me the strange squiggles etched across both invitations. I examined mine with a hammering heart. Kayla was right. They weren't squiggles at all. They were *pictograms*—the same eerie script as the Tomb.

I swallowed. "So you're saying the, uh, Sorcerer left a bone on my doorstep? Some dude trapped inside of a TOMB came by my house this morning and dropped off a package?"

"He's not trapped," Kayla whispered. "Not anymore."

"Huh?"

"You really don't remember, do you?"

Kayla tugged her silvery hair, looking stressed. I had the idea she was doing some very quick thinking.

"You're a June birthday," she muttered. "I'm December. We're the same grade, but I'm six months older...of course..."

"What's my age got to do with the Sorcerer's Tomb?" I asked.

Kayla looked at me, squinted, then shook her head.

"Forget it," she said. "You're not involved anymore. It's me he wants. He's awake and he knows what I did. If I don't stop him now, bad things will happen. Will *keep* happening," she added, with a glance at the bone piles.

I followed her eyes. The bones were flopping even faster now. They slurped through the slime that oozed off their ghoulish, gray-and-brown shapes.

My skin bristled. How long until they reformed into Creeps? Was it really safe to stick around them? And why were their movements speeding up all the sudden?

"Craig, keep an eye on the boys," Kayla ordered. "Whatever happens, don't let Arlo inside of the Tomb."

"Understood!" Stetler tightened his grip on my arm.

Kayla turned her back to us. She gripped her bone invitation, jabbing it toward the Tomb's empty slot.

"Kayla, wait!" I cried. "You don't have to—OW!"

Stetler squeezed. I felt my loose elbow tickle my bicep.

"Stop wriggling!" he spat. "I don't want to hurt you."

"Yes, you do," I growled.

Stetler sniffed. I felt his vice grip abruptly relax.

"Better, Freak? Now stop squawking."

As he spoke, a blinding light burst from the Tomb. Red and silver combined in a glimmering archway as the pictograms brightened like flames.

"Wow," whispered everyone.

The Tomb started shaking. There were rumbles beneath the archway as the heavy stone door slid away, revealing the chamber within.

Eerie red light filled the widening gap.

All our jaws dropped. Even Kayla's.

It looked like a portal to another world. The light inside was pulsing and throbbing, and a musty smell filled our nostrils.

More rumbles. The corridor walls started shaking.

"Something's wrong," I gasped. "The corridor, I think it's collapsing!"

"He's coming," Kayla whispered.

Behind her, the Tomb door had started to seal itself. The entrance was shrinking rapidly.

Kayla touched the brim of her hat, looking back at me. The eerie light of the Tomb flowed past her shoulders and through the gap in her knees. She'd never looked more courageous, not ever.

"Don't follow," she hissed.

And she ran through the archway.

29

THERE WAS NO TIME to gape. We had bigger problems than Kayla's insanity. You see, I was wrong. The corridor wasn't collapsing.

It was filling with bones.

"Go!" Stetler barked. "Slip round the bones! Make a run for it!"

He let go of my arm. I stared at him. Years of torment and bullying flashed before my eyes.

Was this a trick? Stetler couldn't be...*helping* me?

Horrible clicking sounds rang in my ears. Bones were surging out of the wall crack. They piled up in the corridor, slurping like soup as they re-absorbed all the bones Stetler smashed.

My heart was shaking like a popcorn bag.

"Go!" Stetler urged. "Before the bones clog your only escape!"

He shoved Darius and me in front of him.

"W-What about you?" I stammered.

"Freaks first!" Stetler barked. "Slip past the bones and keep running. I'll be right behind y—"

His words were cut off by an extremely loud RAW-WWR! from inside of the Tomb, followed by earsplitting screams.

Stetler's shark-like eyelids flew wide. "Kayla!" he cried, turning heel even faster than Superman.

Truth.

You know how some NFL guys take ballet to improve their speed and reaction time? I think Stetler must've gotten a head start on that. Before I could scream, he'd whipped around like a living tornado, flown backward and squeezed his huge chest through the miniscule gap in the Tomb's sliding door.

THUMP!

The Tomb door slammed shut. The eerie light faded as the gleam drained away from both gates, leaving the item slots empty. Only the quivering torches remained.

And the bones.

The huge blob of clinking and chittering bones that stood between Darius and me and escape.

A dazed look passed between us. We were both thinking the same thing:

What! WHAT! WHAT!!!!

But we couldn't be thinking that. Not with zombie bones pressing in on us. Stetler was right. We had to get past them.

"On the count of three," I told Darius.

But too late. He was already running.

"Oh-God, oh-God, oh-God!"

Darius's high-pitched squeaks filled the corridor. He edged around the bones with quick, splashing steps. I watched his bookbag disappear behind the bone pile, apparently reaching the other side safely. Heart racing, I sucked in a breath.

There was nothing else for it.

And okay, I'll admit, a part of me was praying the zombie bones would act like they did in the river and shy away from me. Because that would be great.

But they didn't. They *lunged.*

"Aaaahhh!" I screamed, pinning my back to the wall, as skeletal hands burst from the bone mass and grabbed me. Icy claws gripped my clothes, dragging me back to the bone pile.

Join us, they seemed to say. *Merge! Merge!*

"Noooo!" I moaned. "Stoppp! Get away from me!"

But how could I stop them? I dug in my heels, but I felt my feet sliding closer, too weak to resist. Ice water flooded my veins. My heart froze in horror and shock.

Then came a SNAP! as my sleeve ripped in two.

Then a SQUISH! as my flexible arm wriggled loose.

Momentum from my escape sent me lurching sideways. I staggered along the wall and into the open corridor. My lungs gasped with cold and surprise.

I did it, I thought. *I reached the other side.*

An icy hand touched my neck and I screamed.

"Aaaaahhhh!"

"Arlo, dude! You made it!"

Darius pulled me into a hug. His clothes were soggy and cold, and his blue Jansport bookbag had a big, toothy hole in the seam. Cine-Blocks were spilling onto the floor, looking like weird Frosted Flakes.

Darius stooped to grab them.

"No time," I hissed. "We've got to keep moving!"

Instead of listening, Darius pulled out his cell phone.

"Are you crazy?" I said.

My best friend's eyes glimmered. "If I go down, I'm going down with the greatest movie footage in history stored on my phone. I'll be famous!"

"You'll be dead!" I cried.

But judging by the dreamy look on his face, Darius wasn't listening. His brain was trapped in director's mode.

I tried tugging his arm. He resisted. I tugged his arm again. I had a really firm grip this time, so I felt the exact moment his body went stiff.

"Indiana Jones," Darius whispered.

"Huh?" I said. "What are you—?"

"INDIANA JONES!" he screeched. Then, slipping my clutches, he turned heel and raced up the corridor, his cell phone held high and reversed. Still recording.

By that point I couldn't resist. I turned around.

You might remember the opening scene of *Indiana Jones and the Raiders of the Lost Ark*. This giant rock gets released and chases Indy down a tunnel. He barely survives.

It's only one of the greatest movie scenes ever.

Ask anyone.

So what if I told you the zombie bone pile had spun itself into a zombie bone BOULDER, like in *Indiana Jones?* And what if this humongous, real-life boulder that was double my height had started to roll at us?

Roll at us.

"RUN!" I shrieked.

"No duh!" said Darius, about a mile ahead of me.

So I ran. No, I *flew* up the corridor. My wide eyes swept the walls, searching for some kind of exit. I could hear the sickening CRUNCH! of the boulder behind me.

My heart hammered. Adrenaline pumped through my ears. And I have to say, it felt *good.*

The more I ran, the more my life flashed before my eyes. My *Indiana Jones* life. I kept imagining ME, Dr. Arlo Vreeland, taking the Harrison Ford role and escaping the boulder at the very last second, just like the scene in the movie.

I'm Indiana Jones, I thought crazily. *I'm the hero!*

I'd never run so fast in my life. My legs swung like pistons. Not the Detroit Pistons. Way faster. Like, it wasn't even a chase. I was burning this stupid boulder.

Then came a horrible SLURP!

And I suddenly remembered why I'd never run so fast before.

My knees squished. My ankles bent like elastic.

I crashed.

I fell flat on my face and lay still.

30

THE BOULDER WAS COMING. Huge rumbles shook through the floor. I pictured all those bones spinning round, or whizzing out the sides like bone shrapnel.

A giant pricker bush crossed with a steamroller.

Crossed with ice cubes.

Not great. Not the best way to die.

I slammed my palms on the floor. I had to move. Now.

But too late. I felt the icy grip of the bone boulder seizing my arms. Flinging me onto my—

"Got—you," wheezed Darius.

He hauled me to my feet. I stared at him. Then I stared at the boulder behind us. It pinballed between the dark walls. It was enormous. And...slow.

It came at us like an elderly jogger.

My smile faded as I realized I *still* couldn't outrun it.

"My ankles," I gasped.

"No sweat, dude, I got you." Darius hooked his arm across my shoulders. "Three-legged race on the count of...GO!"

"GO?"

"GO!"

"Aahhhh!" we both yelled, taking off. I didn't bother mentioning that *both* my ankles were busted. I just leaned left, shoving most of my weight onto Darius.

Somehow, we limped forward.

The boulder approached. We kept limping.

"You're filming this—aren't you?" I panted.

"I'll boost the frame rate—at home," Darius wheezed. "Make it look like—we're running."

Step by step, the corridor shrank, until a stone archway loomed ahead of us, nice and skinny.

An exit.

My heart lifted. I pumped my legs even harder. But not Darius. He suddenly dug in his heels. There was an awful lurch as we jerked to a stop beneath the archway. I swear my ankles almost shot out my toes.

"We can't stop here!" I cried. "THE BOULDER!"

"Just for a second," Darius insisted. "We have to get this boulder on film. *We have to*. We'll slip through the archway right after. The boulder won't be able to fit. Now where's my zoom button? Ugh. These touch controls stink once your fingers go numb."

Darius fiddled with his cell phone.

"It's getting closer!" I yelled.

"Almost got it—"

There was a THUMP! and a shudder of movement.

"It's here!" I squeaked.

Darius was still bent across his phone screen. "Zoom, you stupid app. PINCH. TO. ZOOM!" He started jabbing his fingers at random.

PLUNK!

The cell phone slipped from his hand. It hit the floor and went black. So did the corridor. Darkness fuzzed our eyes as the boulder rolled on.

"Where's my phone?" Darius wailed. "I can't see it!"

He stabbed his hands at the floor, looking panicked. I kept my eyes straight ahead. They were slowly adjusting.

"Darius," I said nervously.

"Help me, Arlo! All our footage is on there!"

"Darius!" I hissed. "Turn around!"

A pair of glowing red dots lit the darkness behind him. There were strange juddering noises as the boulder shook dangerously. It seemed to have stopped rolling.

So what was it doing?

And what was DARIUS doing? He stood frozen between me and the eye lights, his outstretched hand on the floor, as if caught between two separate actions.

I knew he wanted his phone back. But he'd never make it. Even if he found it right now, he still had to pocket it, scurry back to me, lean our shoulders together, and help me limp through the archway.

Or maybe he didn't.

My heart chilled as I realized that Darius still had plenty of time to find his missing phone with all its world-famous footage...*if he ditched me.* No way could the boulder catch up to him running alone.

Me or the movie.

Which would Darius choose?

31

MY NERVES ITCHED WITH DREAD. Darius had dropped to his knees. He was frantically sweeping the floor for his cell phone. Ignoring me.

Eerie red light filled his eyeballs.

It's just a reflection, I told myself. *Darius hasn't turned into a zombie. The Sorcerer CAN'T be controlling him.*

Right?

I held my breath as Darius's body went stiff like a puppet. I knew something had happened. He'd reached a sudden decision.

Or received a command, I thought darkly.

My heart hammered. Almost too quickly, his pudgy neck swiveled. His arms and legs bent unnaturally as an iron grip clutched my shoulders. Darius's big, booming, bullfrog-like voice yelled, "C'mon!"

And we limped through the archway.

It wasn't even that hard.

"What about your phone?" I asked.

"Didn't find it," said Darius. "Not important."

I felt a rush of warmth in my heart. *Thank you, Darius.*

Still limping, I raised my phone for a light. Believe it or not, the boulder *still* hadn't rolled. It was shaking like an egg that was about to hatch.

CRACK!

The enormous bone boulder exploded. Bones pinged off the ceiling and walls as a monstrous skull tumbled onto the floor. Just a skull. Its huge eye lights were burning like flames. Glaring back at us.

No. Glaring at me. My whole body trembled.

Loose bones were creeping back toward the skull. There were slurping sounds as they pushed up around it. I couldn't see what they were doing. It was dark, and most of the light was blood-red.

Suddenly the skull jumped a couple of feet in the air. Then a couple more feet. Bones swelled beneath it like hills, emitting sharp clicks as they bent into all kinds of shapes.

I saw ghoulish gray ribs; cervical vertebrae; and yes, a big sternal plate.

"It's building a body," I whispered.

Was this the Sorcerer's power? Is that why Kayla broke into his tomb? To stop his evil bone army?

RAAWWWRR!

The half-finished monster spread its jaws in a roar that sent chills down my neck.

"Keep moving!" I hissed. "Through the archway!"

But Darius moved the other direction. There was a silver flash as he pulled something out of his bookbag.

A cell phone.

He tapped the dusty screen twice, then beamed as the camera app booted right up.

"Always bring a backup," he cackled. There was a wild gleam in his eye. "Cover me, Arlo. I'm going in for the money shot."

"Cover you? COVER YOU?" I took a gasping breath. "You're insane!"

"No, I'm a director. And this is the shot of a lifetime!"

"But...but there's no footage! We lost it!"

Darius just grinned. He looked crazier than ever! Had the Sorcerer's zombie magic possessed him? Or should we blame planet Spielberg?

Darius easily avoided the hand I reached out. He slipped through the archway, toward the blazing red light of the skeleton. I didn't follow him out. Are you nuts?

Crouched beneath the archway, I tested my ankles. There were faint squishing sounds, but no slurps, plus I didn't fall over.

My bones were firming up again. I could walk!

I took a last look at Darius, cringed, felt a shiver of fear, then turned and set off in the other direction.

"I'll, uh, search the exhibit!" I called over my shoulder. "Just in case something goes wrong and we need to make a quick geta—"

"WAAAAHHHYYY!" shouted Darius.

His bookbag slammed my back like a rocket.

"It's got spikes!" he shrieked. "And a tail! A – A cannonball tail!"

THUMP! A massive force slammed the archway. I didn't dare turn around. I kept my eyes on my shoes.

One foot after another, I told myself, veering round the exhibits. We were in a vast hall of silver and gold. "EGYPTIAN HORRORS," said a banner I ducked underneath.

Yep, I thought. *Sounds like Uncle Leo, all right.*

Darius followed behind. His bookbag dug at my spine as he backpedaled frantically. He wouldn't take his eyes off the creature that chased us.

"It crossed the archway!" he wailed. "Oh God…It's getting taller!"

CRUNCH! "It bit a mummy in half, dude!"

BOOOM! "It smashed a sarcophagus!"

Darius's play-by-play account echoed over the hall, accompanied by footfalls and shattering glass. Tremors shook through the floor. Icy air ripped my lungs; they heaved frantically, struggling to breathe.

I *still* didn't look back. I swerved, ducked and dived. Well, I did the walking equivalent. Did you know speed-walking is an Olympic sport? Just then, I felt like I was smashing the world record.

But it wasn't enough.

The footfalls drew closer. Granite sculptures exploded. A copper amulet skipped past my leg. Darius's voice became a single loud shriek.

"CREEEEEEPOSAAAAURUUUS!"

"No way," I blurted out.

"CREEEEPPPP! CREEEEPPPP!"

Just ignore him, I thought, as my eyes swept the walls. Where were the exits? My heart hammered. For a split-second, I considered doubling back through the archway. But no way could we make it. Even if we did, we'd be sitting ducks in the corridor that dead-ended at the Sorcerer's Tomb.

What was going on? Had I missed a door somewhere?

CRUNCH!

A sudden noise almost blew out our eardrums.

"Do something!" Darius squeaked. "That golden cat statue could've been ME!"

I scanned the walls again. This time, I felt a sudden thrill in my chest. A burst of wild inspiration.

"This way!" I cried, steering us toward a corner. A five-foot-tall Anubis statue stood alone on a pedestal. That's the dog-headed guy. God of death.

Not the smartest choice, looking back.

Darius and I darted behind the Anubis.

"We're done for!" Darius whined. "The Creep is going to find us. H-He'll smash us!"

"Stay calm," I said. "I've got a plan for this. Trust me."

There was a RAWWR! as the bone creature spotted us. Heavy bone feet staggered forward.

They were big. Bigger than I thought.

I jerked my head to the side. "We jump on three," I said shakily. "O-One…Two…"

I saw the shadow of a cannonball tail sweeping down—

"THREE!"

32

THERE WAS A DEAFENING SMASH.

The Anubis statue caught a terrible blow. Its dog head popped off like a firework as its human body flew backward and punched a hole in the wall.

It was a miracle my bones didn't squish and collapse. But they didn't. I'd dived just in time. Darius landed hard right beside me. We held our breath until, finally, the footsteps retreated. The creature must've thought it had finished its mission.

"Oh-God, oh-God, oh-God," said Darius. He eyed the newly-formed crack in the wall. Bones were gushing out in steep waves.

"I knew it!" I cried. "There's a bone river inside of the walls. That's what we'll use to escape!"

There wasn't much time. Even as we spoke, bones were piling up in the gap. I grabbed Darius by his bookbag straps and helped him onto his feet.

"We need to hurry," I said. "We have to reach the river before that...*thing* figures out we're alive."

"We'll never make it," said Darius. "There's too many bones. We won't fit!"

He had a point. Huge stacks of slithery, gray-and-brown bones were now clogging the wall crack.

I inhaled a breath. "We can still do it. The bones from the river don't like me. I'll go first. They'll cut a path for us."

I hope, I thought privately.

There was a RAWWWR! from the other end of the hall. Eerie light slashed a line through the gloom, turning our vision blood-red, as huge footsteps rattled the floor.

Time was up. We'd been spotted.

I grabbed Darius by his bookbag straps.

"Now!" I cried, leaping into the bones.

Did I know for sure the bones would retreat? Nope. Just like I didn't know if the bone river was flowing behind the wall or if the Anubis statue could smash a hole for us if the creature attacked it. I was working on hunches and guesswork, trying to stick the puzzle pieces together before my bones collapsed or the skeleton stomped us.

Or clawed us. Or swallowed us whole.

I was scared. Big time. I showed a brave face to Darius, but on the inside, my nerves felt electric. I kept imagining that awful skull snapping down on my head. I knew exactly what sound it would make. Not a CRUNCH! but a SQUISH!

Darius and I pushed toward the wall. Bones were still streaming out of it, flinging huge gobs of slime in our faces. Man, I really hoped this would work.

The first bone did a flip when I touched it. I sprang backward, barely ducking in time. My heart was pounding like crazy. But it didn't need to be. That one flying leap started a chain reaction across the bone pile. There were frantic clicking and slurping sounds as the bones felt my presence and scampered away.

But why? Why would they do that?

Who cared!

My steps quickened. I suddenly felt like Moses parting the sea in the Bible story. It was seriously cool.

RAAWWRR! And also totally nuts!

The bone creature was right on our heels. Was it really a *Creeposaurus rex?* Were there fangs in its mouth? Was it…*gulp*…forty-feet long? I didn't dare turn around. I never wanted to see those eye lights again.

As I rushed forward, there was a CLINK! and a gust of icy-cold wind. The creature's teeth came together in a bite that could've gobbled a school bus.

It missed.

A second later, I reached the Anubis statue and swung my legs through the hole it made, praying it led to an exit. What if the inside was plugged with rocks or something?

Please be a river, I thought desperately.

I could hear Darius panting behind me.

"It's here…it's the Creep…and it's—AHHHH!"

He gave a strangled yell—I think we both did—as gravity sent us tumbling over the ledge and into the space between walls. There was a loud SPLASH! where we landed, and a rush of ice-cold adrenaline.

Or maybe that was the slime.

We'd survived. The bone river swept us off like a couple of logs. Pretty soon, the Egyptian Horrors exhibit was a distant memory. The creature's howls faded, too.

Darius and I shared a shivering fist bump. Then the chill of the river took over. Our heads bobbed in the thick, boneless sludge. The river was speeding up, doing all kinds of twists. It was all we could do to keep breathing.

"Roller...coaster..." I gasped.

"Yaaah..." Darius said shakily.

Then came a horrible rushing sound.

"DRROOOPPP!" we both yelled, as the river spun us into a drop steeper than anything I'd been on at Six Flags.

I think my heart trampolined off my pelvis.

"AAAHHHHH!" I screamed.

"AAAAHHHH!" shouted Darius.

Our bodies shot down the tunnel, spinning crazily, getting pulled into sharp swerves and loops, until at last we floated into what looked like a cul-de-sac.

The end of the river, I realized.

My brain flew back to the first time we'd entered the bone river. I remembered how badly I'd hoped to explore it. To ride the flow to the end. To find answers.

What was the link between me and the bones? I now knew the Sorcerer's Tomb was involved. Kayla had all but confirmed it. But how? What did she know that I didn't?

He's not trapped. Not anymore.

What was that supposed to mean? Even if the Sorcerer existed, even if he escaped from the Tomb (or whatever), why was it Kayla's job to stop him?

And why Stetler? said the voice in my head.

Ugh. Stetler. *Not as 'Ugh' as before,* I reminded myself.

The memory of Stetler saving Darius and me, then rushing off to save Kayla, turned my brain into mush.

It just didn't make sense.

THUMP! Out of nowhere, my back hit the floor. I looked around. The river was drying up. Only a thin coat of sludge still remained. Like a slip-'n'-slide.

"Whoaaa!" I yelled. We were spinning round. Skidding out of control toward what looked like the end of the tunnel: a solid steel grate.

"I can't stop!" shouted Darius.

"Put your legs up!" I cried. "Brace for—INCOMING!"

CRUNCH! Darius's shoes struck the grate like twin bricks. There was a creaking sound as the grate tumbled loose and we burst through the gap, dropped six inches and landed hard on a cold tile floor.

A sudden "Aahhh!" rose from every direction. Sitting up, I saw my classmates' wide eyes staring back at me.

We were in a small and dimly-lit auditorium. Five rows of seats formed a semi-circle around a white screen connected to a laptop on battery power. A sea of cell phone lights swung from Darius and me to the person in charge, who was standing up front.

Not Ms. Wellington. Not Mrs. Fawcett, either.

He was a man in a tweed coat and jeans, wearing a half-angry, half-baffled expression beneath his fossil-print necktie.

"Arlo?" he said, squinting.

I stared at him.

"DAD?"

33

DAD BLINKED HIS EYES. He didn't cry out in alarm. He didn't mention my soaked clothes or the grate that Darius's feet had knocked loose. Could he even *see* the grate? I wasn't sure. He kept squinting and rubbing his eyes.

Like I said, it was dark.

"Hurry and take a seat, Arlo," Dad said. "You're interrupting my lecture."

He waved at his laptop. It was plugged into some kind of projector.

Huh?

"I don't understand," I said. "I thought you taught college today. You even gave me that bone packet. Why are you here?"

"Leo," Dad said wearily. "Your uncle calls me up, claims there's a crisis at the museum. Come quick, he says, before your *Diplodork* drops its cranium onto its chevrons. It's *Diplodocus*, Leo. *Diplodocus!* So I come rushing over—that's MY *Diplodocus*, even if I haven't seen so much as a rib since Leo got hold of it—and then guess what happens? A blackout! A police barricade! That blasted thunderstorm chases me into the museum. The door locks behind me. I'm trapped! It's a miracle I found my way here."

He waved at the auditorium seats, where the rest of my class was holed up.

"Figured I'd give my lecture while we wait for the storm to pass. Spent all night writing it. At least someone ought to enjoy it. Now sit, Arlo, will you? This laptop charge won't last forever."

I stared in amazement.

Couldn't Dad see I was covered in sludge? Soaking wet? Shivering?

No. He was too busy tapping his laptop. A giant bone diagram filled up the screen.

"*Plateosaurus*," I blurted out.

"Precisely, Arlo. Good guess!"

Didn't need to guess, I thought irritably.

My brain was a mess. I wanted to pull out Dad's packet of bone diagrams and hand it back to him, but with circles for every bone I found missing. I wanted to tell Dad the truth about the Sorcerer's Tomb and the secret river that flowed behind the museum walls, which was stealing bones from all Uncle Leo's exhibits.

Yes, even *Plateosaurus* bones. Especially those.

Then I wanted to tell how I'd TRAVELED the river— escaped from a huge suit of armor—dodged Mini Creeps—then stumbled into what looked like their hideout: The Sorcerer's Tomb.

Had Dad ever heard of that exhibit? Did he know what was hidden inside?

I cleared my throat loudly, preparing to speak. But then my jaw sort of hung there. A dizzy feeling came over me.

The missing *Creeposaurus rex* skeleton…the one that was kind of, sort of, very possibly chasing us…could Darius and I really claim to have found it?

Or had IT found US?

What if it was STILL after us? Could it travel the bone river and rebuild itself in the packed auditorium? Could it speed-run the corridors and come bursting through the front entrance?

My eyes swept the room in a panic. All my classmates were slumped in their seats. They were frowning or laughing or playing games on their phones. I suddenly imagined their shocked faces when the auditorium doors were thrown wide by a forty-foot, serpent-fanged—

"CREEP!" I squealed, as something massive bit down on my arm. I looked up and saw Mrs. Fawcett's huge hand digging into my bicep. She held Darius, too.

"Found 'em!" she grunted. "The runaways!"

There was a stab of eerie red light. It was so sudden, I almost cried out again. But it was just Ms. Wellington scurrying over.

"Oh thank heavens!" she cried, as she clicked off her laser light. "That's two found. Three to go. One of the twins got separated during the blackout. And Erik ran off straightaway. Couldn't catch him. And we just realized KAYLA is missing. The poor thing, she must be petrified!"

"Not exactly," I muttered.

"Did you happen to see them, boys?" Ms. Wellington said hopefully.

I glanced sideways at Darius.

"Stetler," he blurted out. "Stetler wasn't part of your count. Is he back yet?"

The color drained from Ms. Wellington's face. She spun around in a circle, casting wild looks across the auditorium.

"FOUR!" she gasped. "FOUR are missing, not three!"

My skin slurped as Mrs. Fawcett released me. She and Ms. Wellington huddled up by the door to discuss the situation. A nasty popping sound echoed behind them.

"Bad stomach," Mrs. Fawcett moaned.

Darius and I gagged all the way to our seats.

WITH THE CHAPERONES on high alert, Darius and I had no way of escaping Dad's lecture to look for Kayla and Stetler. And even if we could, I wasn't sure that I wanted to.

Because what could I do? I couldn't outrun the bones. I couldn't unlock the Sorcerer's Tomb and save Kayla. Yes, I had a bone to slot into the Bone Gate, but I didn't have that red thing I'd seen in the Heart Gate. I had no idea where to find one, either.

It was hopeless.

A hero wouldn't give up, said the voice in my head. *A hero would risk his life to save the woman he loved.*

WHOA, I thought. *That's the script talking. That's Dr. Arlo Vreeland and Dr. Hannah Yacob from the movie. It's not real. It's not ME.*

I glanced at Darius. His eyes were narrowed and tense. He was scrolling through his backup cell phone as if his whole life depended on it.

All the while, Dad's voice droned across the auditorium.

"Until recently, it was widely believed that dinosaurs were cold-blooded descendants of lizards. Now, however, we are quite certain they were warm-blooded descendants of birds. Many likely had feathers."

Yeah, yeah, I thought. I'd heard this sort of thing a billion times during dinner.

"By digging up bones buried deep in the Earth and comparing them to the bones of existing species, we can infer many things about the Earth's past inhabitants. The fossil record is an extremely powerful tool. And much of it started right here, on the very ground where you sit! The Museum of, um, *Natural History*—ridiculous name—currently stands on top of the world's biggest boneyard. I spent years of my life digging in the pits and ravines we constructed, and I owe my career to the discoveries I made on this very ground. *Plateosaurus. Diplodocus. Tyrannosaurus rex.*"

Dad gave a dry chuckle.

"I see a few of you don't believe me."

Talk about understatement. Barely anyone was paying attention. Even I looked away as Dad stopped the lecture and tapped some more on his laptop.

The light flickered, and gasps from the crowd sent my head jerking up again. Everyone was staring up at the projector screen. Dad's lecture slides were replaced by a picture of a wiry young man in a tight leather harness. He wore a belt of steel tools and was rappelling down the side of the cliff like a trained mountaineer.

"Indiana Jones!" cheered the class.

"Is that really you?" someone chirped. "Do you swear?"

"Who's that kid on your back?" asked another.

Dad's stubbly face broke into a grin like I hadn't seen in ages. His once-tired eyes lit with mischief.

"Got in trouble with Mrs. Vreeland for that one," Dad chuckled. "That's my son, Arlo. I used to take him on digs with me. He was a bit young for it. Not sure he remembers my cool years. So tragic!"

Dad beamed at the projector screen.

"Correction!" he said suddenly. "This one's not Arlo, is it? Hah! It's his little friend, Kayla Caine! I forgot she had red hair back then. Now there was a natural if I ever saw one. The Tiny Tomb Raider, we used to call her at camp! She and Arlo were inseparable. Ah, those were the days. Which reminds me! Has anyone ever told you kids…the legend of the Sorcerer's Tomb?"

34

EXCITED WHISPERS FILLED the auditorium. Dad's stubbly face lit up even more.

"Oh, they *haven't?*" he said. "Well then! Sit back and enjoy, because this one's a doozy. A bit of local folklore you won't find in books!"

Dad's eyes were glittering now. He looked about twenty years younger, almost kid-like, as he beamed from the top of the stage.

I couldn't look away. Not even to trade looks with Darius. Anxiety kept me glued to my seat, shaking with anticipation. What would Dad say? What did he know that I didn't? Judging by the buzz of noise all around me, I wasn't alone in my questions.

"No one knows how the legend began," Dad announced. "When my team and I first settled the Cretaceia dig site, a little over seven years ago, the tale seemed to appear out of nowhere. As if it arose from the very fossils themselves!"

Dad smiled spookily.

"As you may be aware, the Cretaceia region of Triosset Township was left wild and undeveloped until very recently, when our instruments detected an extremely high level of fossil-rich rock. My team and I were over the moon at the time. We couldn't believe our good luck! Though in light of events, we must ask ourselves…was it too good to be true? Did this old land carry with it…*a curse?*"

Dad's shining eyes swept the room. He seemed to be enjoying himself. But not me. I held my breath as he fiddled his fossil-print necktie.

"Rumors spread from the moment we set up our tents. This land was protected, they said. The fossils were not ours to extract. No. Another figure had claimed them, the so-called Sorcerer, whose tomb lay buried at the core of our dig site.

"According to legend, whoever disturbed the Sorcerer's slumber would receive *Umklasum*. Yes. *Umklasum*. Now I know what you're thinking: what language is that? No one knows. Does *Umklasum* refer to a curse? A reward? Someone's pet *Pterodactyl?* The word was never traced to any known culture. It's as impenetrable as the Basque language! A sort of spoken-word Linear B. You can't even Google it. But I digress!"

Dad grinned at us.

"In all likelihood, the Sorcerer's Tomb is a myth. Some person's idea of a joke. Or perhaps a disgruntled local's attempt to frighten us off of the land. Either way, the story spread and grew famous. My team and I knew better than to believe it. Well, most of us. But the kids really loved it."

The laptop screen flashed. A series of images appeared on the wall. Tiny white tents. Men and women in rugged clothes, stabbing chisels at exposed lengths of rock. Then a single large crack in the earth, like a bottomless pit. A sea of warning flags marked the steep edges.

The screen changed again. It showed a five-year-old Kayla Caine with a chisel and tape measure poking out of her cargo shorts. An even tinier individual—*me*—lagged behind, dragging a shovel my arms couldn't lift.

Everyone laughed.

"As I said," Dad went on, "my son Arlo was a bit young. Not sure he understood much. Kayla led him around like a puppy. She was a few months older than Arlo—it matters at that age—and I'm sure she remembers it well. Right, Kayla? Are you with us?"

Dad's eyes scanned the dark auditorium. Ms. Wellington and Mrs. Fawcett were shifting uncomfortably.

"Oh, nevermind then," Dad laughed.

He started showing more images. Nearly all were of me. Stuff I barely remembered. I saw myself knee-deep in fossils. Tapping chisels with a tiny mallet. Doing snow-angels in the dirt and rising all muddy.

And in every frame, there was Kayla beside me, doing everything I was doing, but better. More adult-like. I don't know how you could tell. You just could.

"We had great fun pretending to look for the Sorcerer's Tomb every day," said Dad. "Arlo and Kayla were full of excitement. They clocked in at six a.m. every shift, same as us! There's Arlo with his pointing trowel. Ah, and

there's Kayla. Believe me, you didn't mess with Kayla during a dig. She swung that tape measure around like a bull-
whip!"

More laughter.

"Needless to say, we found enough bones on our trip
to fill several museums. Or one very big one!"

Dad looked around at the walls, sighing wistfully.

"If you ask me, the construction of this museum was a
national tragedy. I have no doubt there are fossils still buried beneath us. I simply do not understand who approved
the construction plans, or what their motives might be.
Case in point: they hired my brother, Leo, to run the place.
That's the level of intellect we are dealing with. You might
remember Leo as the man who used to deliver pizza to
your doorstep. Cold pizza. Thirty minutes too late."

Dad cleared his throat loudly.

"Nevertheless," he said, "the museum's sudden ap-
pearance does leave one question unanswered. *What became
of the Sorcerer's Tomb?*

"Some say the Tomb is still lurking beneath us. Still
undiscovered. Still waiting to bestow its *Umklasum* on
some hapless explorer. As for me, I was forced into early
retirement. A desk job! There were simply too many bones
to sort, and none left to dig. Plus a little incident I would
prefer not to—*Ah.*"

Before Dad could finish, the screen changed again. A
wide image showed several adults grouped around the
warning flags, looking tense and upset as they peered
down the chasm below.

Behind his laptop, Dad chuckled nervously.

"Ah, forgot this was in here. Not my finest hour. So, uh, how to explain? You see, the kids got a tad overeager at one point. In their hunt for the Tomb, my son crept a little too close to the warning flags. Kayla, too. They, er, fell in the hole. No one knew. Couldn't find them for hours!"

"Hours?" said a pair of shocked voices.

Dad's face reddened. "Er, it was minutes, I'm sure. Probably seconds! Right. More importantly, we found the kids in the end. Pulled them out! Little Kayla even brought back a souvenir. She was so proud of it. Hmm, let's see if I still have the slide…"

A hush fell over the room as Dad bent toward his laptop. He was clicking around, tapping keys. And then—

"Whoaa!"

A burst of light filled the dark auditorium.

Eerie red light.

The table supporting Dad's laptop started creaking and shaking. Ripples in the projector screen seemed to spread to the floor.

My whole body rang with alarm.

It's here, I thought crazily. *It found us!*

More glowing light filled the room. Then came a horrible, hideous, bone-shaking, "RAAWWWRR!"

35

FEAR FLOODED INTO ME. Panicked, I cast around for the source of the roar. Was it Dad's laptop? The empty seats? The fallen grate where the bone river—

No. Nothing.

Finally, I glanced at the exit door. An eerie light splashed the wood as the roaring continued. My heart trembled. Then, just as I expected a forty-foot Creep to come bursting in on us, snapping the door like a toothpick, a voice echoed:

"Paging Dr. Fossil! Dr. Fossil. Dr. Fossil."

I spun toward the stage. Dad's cell phone was going nuts. It was beeping and buzzing, causing the tiny wood table to quake.

"One moment," said Dad. "Finally got a connection!" He scooped his phone off the table. "Hey? Leo?"

There was a pause. And then—

"Good heavens!" Dad exclaimed. "Leo, where have you *been?* No, I haven't seen my exhibit yet. Can't see two feet in front of my—"

Another pause.

"Dang right I'm annoyed! Seeing my fossils properly assembled and catalogued is the only reason I'm—NO I

WILL NOT 'TAKE A CHILL PILL', LEO! Where are you right now? Leo? Hello?"

Dad thumped his cell phone and groaned.

"Disconnected! The cell service here is a joke. Ugh. He'd better call back..." Silence fell as Dad blinked and looked up at us. "Er, sorry about that. Unavoidable. Now where was I?"

No idea, I thought dizzily. But I knew exactly where *I* was. In a daze. My heart beat like a drum. Eerie red light was spilling across Dad's face and down his fossil-print necktie.

"Ah yes! The survivors!"

Dad jabbed his thumb at the bright-red projector screen. Blazing across it was a photo of Kayla and me.

Mostly Kayla.

No. Mostly that *thing* she was holding. The rock.

We were sitting cross-legged in the dirt, surrounded by pulleys and ropes. The chasm loomed a few feet away. Judging by the adults' shocked looks, I think we'd just been pulled out of it. My expression was blank. Almost dumb.

Kayla was beaming. She clutched a spiky red rock in her fist. Its eerie light swallowed half of the frame, staining everything red, like a sunset.

Like a heart.

Yes. There was no mistaking what the red rock resembled. The voice in my head was practically screaming it.

HEART GATE!

THAT'S THE THING FROM THE HEART GATE!

"I don't believe it," I whispered.

Darius looked up from his cell phone. "Hey Arlo," he said, "doesn't that red rock kind of remind you of—?"

"Yes!" I hissed. "Yes!"

Then I shushed him since Dad was still talking.

"...so thank heavens it worked. We weren't sure the pulleys would hold! So if my team and I look a bit frazzled, *we were*. That was the end of Dig Site Daycare, believe me!"

Dad smiled sheepishly.

"You're probably wondering about the stone in little Kayla's right hand. Bright, isn't it? Seems the computer is struggling to render it. Just tilt your head a bit. That's it. You might have to squint."

Blood thumped in my ears. It felt as if the eerie red light was creeping under my skin. Crawling into me.

"According to our on-site geologist, the rock is common bauxite. A type of aluminum ore. An exemplary specimen, of course—but there's nothing sacred or cursed about sedimentary rock. We let the kids take it home with them. A little parting gift from the Sorcerer! If I recall, Kayla's mother had it carved into something more memorable. Charm bracelets, I think? Or were they necklaces? I never remember—"

Dad's voice cut off as another "RAAWWWRR!" shook the table. He grabbed his cell phone. He practically strangled it.

"It's Leo!" he huffed. "Ugh. Excuse me."

Dad stalked off the stage and through the exit door.

The screen dimmed as a screensaver flashed on Dad's laptop, removing the eerie red glow of the image.

But what if I told you the glow *from inside of my shirt* would replace it?

I couldn't breathe. Couldn't think.

Hooking my thumb beneath my shirt collar, I gripped my ratty charm necklace and flopped it over my collar. A spark of eerie red light flickered over my throat.

Darius gave an audible gasp.

"Dude," he said. "DUDE!"

My lips trembled. I turned to stare at him.

"Dude."

36

DID YOU KNOW THE ANCIENT GREEKS invented the catapult? Ms. Wellington says the Ancient Chinese built their own version, too, called a mangonel. And maybe that's true. But we didn't have a twenty-foot-long Ancient Chinese mangonel blocking our path across the museum.

We had a catapult.

Four of them, actually.

"THIS…IS…SPARTA!" said the banner Uncle Leo pinned up. We were huddled outside the auditorium, in the middle of this weird Ancient Greek Warfare exhibit Uncle Leo cooked up.

On our left stood four giant catapults, their throwing arms cocked and ready to fire.

On our right was the army. The statues. Six rows of marble and bronze figures, called *kouros*, were directly facing the catapults, as if preparing for battle. The semi-darkness made the statues look spookily real.

"It's like a scene out of *Gladiator,*" Darius whispered.

I was about to say no, doofus, it's not, because *Gladiator* is a film about Romans, not Greeks, but I stopped myself.

What's the point? Darius never listens to me, anyway.

He gestured to a gap in the catapults.

"Over there," he whispered. "We need to talk, Arlo. Somewhere teachers can't hear us."

My skin prickled. Did I know what Darius wanted to talk about? Of course I did. But that didn't mean I was happy about it.

I clutched my throat where the charm necklace hung. When Ms. Wellington and the rest of our class headed right, through the statues, Darius and I ducked our heads and went left, toward the catapults.

We almost didn't make it. Mrs. Fawcett must've sniffed us out, because she paused and spun around. Meanwhile, the storm clouds were lifting. Light from the windows flooded into the hall. That meant Darius and I were suddenly, horribly visible.

But so were the Greek *kouros* statues.

Have you ever seen an Ancient Greek statue? Trust me, there's a lot to see in some parts. Like, A LOT.

"Look away!" Mrs. Fawcett shrieked. *"Avert your eyes!"*

She rushed around, trying to cover kids' faces.

Yes. The statues were nude.

APPARENTLY DAD HAD crossed the catapults, too, because we found him hugging the walls, walking fast toward a far-distant archway. His loud voice echoed over the helmet and spear displays.

"No, I didn't ask THE SUIT OF ARMOR for directions, Leo! What on Earth—?"

"What do you mean there's NO MAP?"

"Oh nevermind. It's through here—"

'PAGODA? You named my exhibit JURASSIC PAGODA? That doesn't even—wait a second—what IS this?"

Footsteps echoed as Dad raced through the archway. Then: "LEEEEOOOOOOO!!!"

"I think your dad found his fossils," Darius whispered.

"Yeah," I sighed. "With thirty to forty percent of the bones missing. Plus fangs."

We ducked behind a catapult arm until the yelling died down. It took a minute. Or twelve. And then Darius and I were suddenly, finally, alone.

I blew out a breath. I knew it wouldn't be long before one of the chaperones came looking for us.

Probably Mrs. Fawcett.

I knew she was mad. She seemed to view the missing kids as a personal insult. As if we were the prisoners and she was the prison guard. If she caught Darius and me sneaking off, detention was the least of our problems.

But whatever. Ask me if I cared.

I had bigger worries than Mrs. Fawcett's power trip. Well, one big one.

The necklace. The bauxite.

Hidden beneath my shirt was the key to unlocking the Heart Gate—and with it, the Sorcerer's Tomb.

I pulled the necklace out of my shirt and examined it while Darius filmed a few close-up shots.

"So Kayla had the other necklace this whole time," he mused. "That's interesting. Do you think she knows what the rock is?"

"Duh," I said. "She knew how to open the Sorcerer's Tomb, remember? She knew about the gates. She went LOOKING for them. She brought a full explorer's kit along, too. *And* a bodyguard."

"So Stetler's the muscle?" said Darius.

My lips tightened. "I don't know. Maybe."

The question left me uneasy. I still hadn't figured the whole Stetler thing out. What did Stetler want with the Tomb? Why was he working with Kayla?

No. Why was Kayla working with HIM?

Darius shook his head in amazement.

"Who knew Dr. Hannah Yacob would turn out this awesome? No offense, dude, but she's way cooler than Dr. Arlo Vreeland. Like, it's almost a plot hole."

"Oh shut up."

"Easy, doc. Save your scowl for the camera." Darius grinned. "We're going back to the Tomb, right? We have to. We have to finish the movie."

My heart sank.

"I knew you would say that," I muttered. What's worse was, deep down, I agreed with him. We had to go back.

No, I didn't *want* to see the Tomb again. I didn't want to risk running into that bone creature and dying instantly. I wanted to get the heck out of here!

But some part of me felt weird about leaving Kayla and Stetler on their own. What if they couldn't escape the Tomb? What if the bone creature came back and trapped them? *Or the Sorcerer?*

Could I really just leave them there, when I was the only other person with a chance of unlocking the Tomb?

I squeezed my charm necklace again. Eerie red light filled my knuckles. My stomach twisted.

Like I said, I knew what Darius and I had to do. But that didn't mean I wasn't totally freaked. And it didn't mean I wouldn't still try to talk my way out of it, either.

"We could die," I pointed out.

"We could win the *Grand Prix* at the Shudder Oaks Film Festival," said Darius. His eyes had that invincible, director's-cut gleam again.

I tried a different tactic.

"First of all," I said, "I don't think *Prix* rhymes with *Twix*. Second of all, I think Dr. Hannah Yacob—I mean, Kayla—has a better shot at escaping than us. Remember how prepared she was? She's probably out of the Tomb by now. Safe and sound."

I hope, I thought privately.

"Third of all," I said, with a knot in my chest, "we can't actually finish the movie. We lost the footage, remember?"

Darius looked at me.

I swallowed.

I knew what losing the movie had cost him. Making movies was his passion.

But I also knew I would've NEVER escaped the bone boulder if Darius hadn't abandoned his dream on the floor, grabbed my shoulder and helped me limp away on my two busted ankles.

He could've grabbed his cell phone and left me there.

He didn't. He rescued me.

My insides squirmed guiltily. I suddenly realized I'd never thanked him for doing that. Not properly. Not enough.

So that's what I did. I tried, anyway. I explained how grateful I was. How, in my head, I could still picture the moment he made up his mind. How his arms and legs froze. His eyes glimmered. And he spun around, gripped my shoulder and—

"Oh, that!" Darius interrupted. "Yeah, I *had* just remembered something, actually. My cloud backup drive! Everything I film gets uploaded to my online account automatically. That must've been the moment when I realized finding the phone didn't matter. It'd be quicker to ditch it and pull out the spare."

Darius beamed at me.

"I spent most of the lecture downloading footage onto my backup phone. I was so worried the connection would drop, but it didn't. I guess my cell plan is better than your dad's, huh? Arlo? Arlo?"

I just stared at him.

Because how do you answer that?

37

BEFORE WE GO ANY FURTHER, I have to be honest: I've been dreading this chapter.

But it's fine now. I think I finally know how to do it.

You see, there's another game I like to play.

No, it's not Jenga.

The game is called Two Truths and a Lie, and I want to play it right now. I'm going to say three things about my book. Two things are true. One is a lie.

Can you guess the lie on my list?

#1 – A lot of scary stuff is about to happen *right now*.

#2 – All of it *actually* happened. It won't be made up.

#3 – The events in chapter one…*ahem*…also happened.

Tick. Tick. Tick. Got your answer? Okay, so it wasn't that tough. #3 is the lie. Kind of.

Look, it's hard writing books. I'm in sixth grade. I don't always know what I'm doing. Sometimes I get overexcited. And yeah, I start making things up.

I never lie about big things. I swear. It's just…I want people to read this. It's an important true story. It could happen to YOU. So when I started writing it, I was afraid people wouldn't believe me. I wanted to cut to the chase, you know? Zombie bones. Bone rivers. Bone boulders.

THE SORCERER'S TOMB.

But I didn't do it. I couldn't. I knew if I wrote the truth on page one, people would stop reading and call me a liar. They'd throw my book in the sink! (Toilet? Trash can?)

So I started slow. I focused on the missing bones and the mystery of Uncle Leo's museum. Where did the museum come from? How did Uncle Leo get picked as Director? Seriously—who hired him?

(More on that later).

But while I wrote all that down, I kind of, sort of, maybe somehow implied there were secret passages in Uncle Leo's museum. Corridors that widened and changed, like the hallways at Hogwarts. And that Darius and I were sneaking down one of them on a wild hunt for the missing Creep bones that Darius spotted.

Well, no. Those were tunnels. Bone rivers.

And we weren't LOOKING for the Creep bones. If anything, we were LOOKING OUT for them.

We were terrified.

The tunnels were how Darius and I sneaked away from our class after the *kouros* incident. They're how we almost froze to death, wading through buckets of sludge as we tromped through the walls. And ultimately, the tunnels were how we found the Sorcerer's Tomb again.

We followed the slime.

Same as Kayla.

THE JOURNEY THROUGH the tunnels was bad. It was more than the cold and the slime, because at every turn, every twist of the labyrinth that secretly ran through the walls, I imagined the *Creeposaurus rex* flying out at us. I saw its huge skull in my mind. Its murderous eye lights. Its fangs that were bigger than yardsticks.

Stay calm, I thought. *You can do this.*

I glanced at Darius. He flashed an icy thumbs-up from behind his cell phone. We trudged on.

Another creepy thing was the bones had gone missing. I don't mean they swerved to avoid me. I mean MISSING.

Just gone.

Not a femur or rib. Not a vertebra.

I had a sneaking suspicion I knew where the bones had retreated to. It only made my stomach twist even more.

Cold seeped through my skin and into my bones. Every part of me shivered and squished as I trudged through the tunnels, choosing turns where the slime trail was thickest.

Fog billowed everywhere, obstructing my vision. So how did I know where to stop?

I saw torches.

Yellow light was leaking through one of the walls. I turned and saw what looked like a person-sized crack, with an ancient stone wall just beyond.

The Sorcerer's Tomb.

We'd arrived.

38

"SO…COLD," I GASPED, tumbling out of the wall crack.

"Can't lift…the camera," said Darius.

We huddled beneath the torches, trying to warm our shaking bodies. The floor was slimy, like the tunnel, but there were no bones in sight.

I gazed at the Tomb.

"It's quiet," I whispered.

The slots beneath the Bone Gate and Heart Gate lay empty and black. No light emerged from the archway that stood in between.

I climbed to my feet, feeling along the stone wall. I don't know what I was searching for. My thumb had just brushed the slot beneath the Heart Gate when—

BOOOM!

The Tomb rumbled. A muffled cry rose from within.

BOOOM! BOOOM!

Tremors shook through the stone. Cobwebs leapt off the wall, flinging soot and dust, as the torches gave a hiss and went out.

Blackout. Then a tiny light cut through the darkness.

I spun around.

Darius's flashlight app swept past my face and up the shaking stone wall. It was a moment before I stopped gasping. I felt like I was in one of those low-budget horror movies where you can't see a thing until the monster jumps out.

Then I realized I actually *was* in a horror movie.

It wasn't a documentary anymore. It wasn't a thrilling adventure starring Dr. Arlo Vreeland, a completely made-up character.

It was horror. Pure horror.

Except I didn't need to pretend there were monsters lurking around in the darkness. I *knew* there were monsters. I'd seen them.

I also knew I was heading straight for their hideout.

The Sorcerer's Tomb.

But why? What kind of person would DO that?

Don't look at me. My brain was totally fried by that point. I felt like a puppet, blindly following the plan Darius and I had laid out. As for what would happen if the Tomb really opened...

Don't ask. Like I said, my mind was a blank.

Finally the rumbles stopped, and I recovered enough to press my ear to the stone. I was listening. Trying to make out the noises inside.

A scream? Hadn't I just heard a scream?

My heart thumped. I wanted to get the heck out of there. But which direction? I didn't want to hang around in the corridor, in case the *Creeposaurus rex* came back. But

I didn't want the Tomb open, either, because who knew what was in there?

Bones, I thought crazily. *Bones from the tunnels.*

But there was nothing else for it.

No heroes to summon. No adults who could help.

I took a deep breath, then slid the bone invitation out of my pocket. I paused before reaching my hand out.

It was a pretty long pause.

C'mon, I told myself. *You got this. Quit stalling.*

I clenched my teeth. There was a soft click as the invitation dropped into the slot. The stone trembled. Silver light flooded into the pictograms across the Bone Gate.

One down, I thought breathlessly.

I crossed the sealed door to the empty slot beneath the Heart Gate, the necklace held tight in my hand. An icy chill bit my palm as I undid the latch and raised it into the air.

My heart hammered. Was I crazy for doing this?

Would it work?

What if Kayla had more of the bauxite than I did? What if she hadn't used the necklace at all? It was a charm necklace from seven years ago. It would be crazy if Kayla still wore it. Right?

You still wear it, I thought.

"Arlo, c'mon," said Darius. "What're you waiting for?"

"R-Right."

I inhaled a breath. It was time to act. Time to finish this.

I squeezed the necklace and, in one fluid move, I reached forward, thrust it into the slot and stepped back, hardly daring to breathe.

Silence. More silence. Then, just as my lungs screamed for air, the Tomb shuddered. Crimson light exploded out of the Heart Gate, across the pictograms and into my eyes.

Into the cold museum air. Into the fierce silver light flaring up from the opposite side of the archway. Then, sooner than I expected—sooner than I was ready for—the Tomb door slid open. Eerie red light wafted out of the archway, like fog.

Something rustled behind me. I whipped around.

Darius was breathing in short, heavy gasps. He looked terrified. He propped his phone on my shoulder, his camera arm shaking beneath it.

Together, we squinted into the fog.

And what did we see?

Nothing at first. The air was so gloomy and red, it was hard for my eyes to adjust. Once they did, though, I started to notice things.

High ceilings. Huge, hulking shapes in the background. And eyes. A sea of piercing red eyes.

Like fiery orbs, the eyes swung to greet us. I counted eight pairs at first. Then fifteen. Then I blinked and saw…*hundreds*. There were eyes everywhere, rising out of the fog on all sides.

"Unghhh," I said helplessly.

"Oh-God, oh-God, oh-God," whispered Darius.

We took a frightened step back. And then—

"Kaaaa-waaahhh!" cried a voice. There was a violent thrashing sound.

THUMP! THUMP! THUMP!

One by one, the eye lights fell dark.

My jaw dropped. Across the fog, I saw two figures huddled together. One of them was built like a boulder with big, swinging arms. The other was smaller. Prettier.

A plastic cowboy hat slid down her ear while pools of sludge and sweat soaked her clothes. Her dark eyebrows scrunched for a moment, then lifted into her hat as she spotted me.

"A-Arlo!" she spluttered. "You…you…"

Yes? I thought eagerly, breathlessly.

I stepped forward.

"BEHIND YOU!" cried Kayla.

My heart jolted. A wave of horror rushed through me.

Because that's when I heard it. A sound like volcanoes erupting inside of my ears—mixed with smoke alarms—and that toilet scene from the *Jurassic Park* movie.

You know the one. Say it with me now.

"RAAAAAAAAAAWWWWWWRRRRRRR!"

39

IT WAS THE CREEPOSAURUS REX. You know it. I know it. Even then, standing frozen in fear inside the Sorcerer's Tomb, I knew the identity of the horrible, forty-foot, crimson-eyed creature that had crept up behind me.

Its icy breath stung my neck. Its massive skull creaked as it entered the archway. And when I finally regained my strength, turning round, I really, really wished that I hadn't.

"Ahhhhhhhhh!" I cried. "AAAAAaaaaaHhHhHHH!"

My knees squished and I crashed to the floor.

The Creeposaurus's jaws opened wide. It could've swallowed me, easy. It could've swallowed Mrs. Fawcett.

No. Our school bus!

A long second passed. I watched those jaws stretch impossibly wide...then they LUNGED.

SKRRRRR! There was a horrible scraping sound. Sparks flew from the skull as it squeezed through the archway, thrusting its snout through the gap.

I closed my eyes.

A massive force gripped my shoulders and pulled. I thought I was dead. I felt a dozen sharp teeth digging into me. Tearing my flesh. Biting holes in my—

Wait. No. That strange force pulled me deeper into the Tomb. Away from the Creep.

Darius? I thought crazily.

I opened my eyes and saw frizzy black hair right beside me. The same force had seized Darius by his bookbag straps. We were BOTH being dragged.

"Over here, Freaks!" barked a voice. "Before that Godzilla thing eats you alive!"

It was Stetler. He flung us behind a mountain of cracked, lifeless bones, then rounded on one of the small, rat-like things flopping out of it.

"KWEEK!" it cried. "KWEEK!"

Stetler cringed.

SMASH! He stomped the bone anyway.

"Disgusting," he said. A shiver ran across his bald head.

I climbed to my feet, looking round. My heart thudded. The *Creeposaurus rex* stood a few steps away, glaring with hungry red eyes. Its huge skull was stuck in the archway.

"Oh thank God," I said.

"It's not over yet," growled a voice. A short, scowling girl in messy clothes and a cowboy hat shuffled over.

"Dr. Hannah!" I cried out.

Kayla stared at me. Her nose twitched.

"Why won't you LISTEN?" she snapped. "Why do you always COME BACK?"

"I, uh…came to rescue you?"

"ARGH!"

Kayla grabbed a fistful of her own hair and started pulling it. I was shocked to see silvery tufts dropping out. They hung in the air, floating next to her hat brim.

"WHY DO YOU KEEP DOING THIS?" she roared.

"D-Doing what?" I said.

But as I spoke, another Creep scurried out of the shadows, making a beeline for Darius. There was a "KWEEK!" and a CRUNCH! as Stetler flattened it under his heel.

"Nice one," Darius gasped.

Stetler gave a tired thumbs-up, then marched off to look for more targets.

Kayla sighed irritably. "We've been stuck here for hours," she said. "We're trying to get over there, of course—"

She pointed to a strange sort of light in the distance, pulsing silver and red.

"A dance floor?" I blurted out.

Kayla ignored me.

"Unfortunately," she said, "there's just too many bones. One step and they come crawling out of the shadows, like rats. We've only faced small ones so far. They must've slipped through a crack somewhere. Or maybe they were already here. I don't know."

She sighed wearily.

"At least we're evenly matched—the bigger bones can't get in, thankfully—but progress is slow. At this rate, we'll never reach the rock before—AHHH!"

There was a loud slurping noise. Panicked, I checked my ankles and knees.

Still intact.

So then…

My eyes flew to the archway. The *Creeposaurus rex* skull was disassembling itself! Jagged teeth fell from its jaw, which itself seemed to flop into pieces—as if the Creep's skull wasn't a single huge bone, but a jumble of other, tinier bones mashed together like plywood.

Like Cine-Blocks.

My heart shivered. A mass of gray-and-brown bones pushed through the archway and into the Tomb. There were suddenly hundreds of living bones in the slime. Maybe thousands!

"I was hoping he wouldn't figure that out," Kayla moaned.

"He?" I said hysterically. "Who is HE?"

Kayla didn't answer. Bones that had crossed the archway were already reforming. Their shrill cried filled the air.

"KWEEK! KWEEK! KWEEK!"

"Mini Creeps!" Darius cried. He fumbled for his cell phone, then uttered a wail as Stetler shoved him aside, out of range of a Creep's lunging talon.

My eyes swung around. The Mini Creeps were everywhere. There were more springing up every second.

SMASH! SMASH! SMASH!

"You! Freak!" Stetler shouted mid-foot stomp. "Come help me!"

I stared at him.

"Not you!" Stetler bellowed. "HIM!"

A huge hand seized Darius by his bookbag straps. Stetler eyed him appraisingly.

"Nice tri's," he said, pinching Darius's arm. "You work out?"

"I…watch *The Karate Kid* a lot," Darius said warily.

It was good enough for Stetler, apparently, because a second later, the two of them stood side by side, squaring off against a huge wave of Mini Creeps.

"Stetler Smash!" shouted Stetler, through slitted eyes.

"S-S-S-Sweep the leg!" Darius screeched, while his outstretched arm aimed his cell phone. Recording the fight.

My jaw had long since fallen open. I just stood there and watched. I almost couldn't believe it.

"Snap out of it!" Kayla yelled. "Arlo! We have to get *there!*" She jerked a hand toward the silver-red platform.

"The dance floor?" I said stupidly.

"No, dummy! That's the Sorcerer's—ugh, nevermind!" She took off running.

"Hannah, wait!" I cried out. "Dr. Yacob! Uh, Kayla!"

I raced after her. I made it two steps before I squished to a halt. I felt a horrible looseness.

Not again, I thought miserably.

Heels swaying, I watched Kayla's mad dash through the Tomb. Darius and Stetler were still fighting. Their battle cries rang in my ears, punctuated by low grunts and the loud CRACK! of Mini Creeps bursting apart.

And where was I? Standing still. Sinking deeper into the floor every heartbeat.

I watched, helpless, as the next line of Creeps avoided Darius's leg, scuttled sideways, and dashed after Kayla. They weren't the only ones. More and more Creeps were emerging. Fangs glinting, they climbed out of shadows. They tore themselves out of the ground, like true zombie warriors.

There were SO MANY. Too many.

Kayla jerked to a stop. Overwhelmed. Half-surrounded.

A blinding light stabbed my eyes. Darius had swung his cell phone around, tracking the course of the Creeps on his camera app, while Stetler's fists waffled uselessly.

The Mini Creeps were ignoring them.

Worse, they were too far away to reach Kayla.

But I'm not, I thought breathlessly.

My heart hammered. This was it. The big moment.

I knew I had to do something. I just didn't know what. Like I said, I'm not a hero. I wish I were (all the time) but I'm not. I wasn't born brave as a lion. No one ever confused me with Indiana Jones or called me The Tiny Tomb Raider when I hung out at dig sites.

I'm not even a good Dr. Arlo Vreeland.

So how was I supposed to save Kayla from a horde of Creepified bones? I watched them surge forward, forming a ring around Kayla's position.

"KWEEK!" they cried. "KWEEK! KWEEK!"

They hopped around, spraying sludge and climbing across each other's backs.

The seconds ticked by. The ring tightened.

More and more bones were joining the fray, turning the ring into a massive blockade, growing steadily thicker and taller.

After about ten seconds, when the ring reached a height of eight feet, I realized my moment had passed.

After twenty seconds, I began to shake uncontrollably.

But it wasn't until a full minute went by, maybe more, that the ring of bones reached its maximum height.

The mass of Creeps started swaying. Slime oozed down the sides in thick gobs, piling up on the floor. There were slurping sounds. Loud snaps and squishes. The walls of the ring teetered dangerously. Then—

KAAAABOOOOOM! They collapsed. They caved in!

"K-K-Kayla!" I cried.

She was gone. Vanished into the bones.

All that remained was a single round object, roughly the size of a church. No, a SCHOOL.

The clump of bones stretched so wide, I could barely see the edge of it. I spread my eyes to the limit. I didn't dare move my feet, but I had to see what had happened. I had to know if Kayla…if she'd actually…

"Unngh!" I gasped loudly.

A girl in the filthiest, nastiest, most sludge-covered hat I'd ever seen came streaking out of the slime, her silver hair gummed to her neck, like a fleece-colored scarf.

Kayla reappeared at my side in an instant.

"K-Kayla," I stammered. "I…I thought you were…"

Kayla bowed her head. Before I could finish, suddenly Stetler was there, hugging her. Then Darius trotted up, making all kinds of noise with his bookbag. Breathless, we pressed our bodies together, forming a trembling and terrified knot. Staring up.

Staring EVERYWHERE.

It was then that I realized the Tomb's extremely high ceilings weren't just for show. They were NEEDED.

The boulder the size of a school had transformed. Like some horrible egg, it had hatched, and in its place sat the biggest dinosaur skull I'd ever seen in my life.

Don't get me wrong. With Dad's job hunting fossils, I'd seen plenty of skulls before, including the biggest on record—a *Pentaceratops*. It's in Oklahoma somewhere. Dad and I stopped to see it on our way to the Mayo Clinic.

Anyway, this skull was bigger.

It made *Pentaceratops* look like a cricket.

It even made the LAST Creeposaurus look wimpy.

Put it this way: if Mini Creeps were Transformers, then this skull was their Megatron. No. This was the thing that ATE Megatron, then went back and ate Galvatron, too.

I watched, trembling, as a fresh wave of bones rushed the skull, welling up underneath it.

Assembling its skeleton.

My heart shivered. Just what sort of skeleton could support a skull like that? How tall would it get? Eighty feet? One hundred?

The thought left me dizzy. I suddenly had no problem understanding how the *Creeposaurus rex* poked its head out the tower window this morning. Looking back, I was lucky it hadn't stretched it neck out and chomped me right then.

Not so lucky anymore, I thought, as its crimson eyes flared. Angry red light split the Tomb like a laser. The glare was so bright, it made the fog from before look invisible.

A set of jaws the size of a two-car garage split apart as its empty throat blazed like a fireball.

Suddenly the skull shifted. It rose in the air.

Teeth like Greek spears clinked together.

Fangs as long as flagpoles curled over our heads.

There was no escape. I knew it as sure as I knew my own bones (well, sixty to seventy percent of them).

An icy hand squeezed my palm.

"I'm sorry I couldn't break the curse for us," Kayla whispered. "I tried, Arlo. I really, really tried."

I had no idea what she meant, and no voice to reply with. My throat clenched with fear.

The *Creeposaurus rex* skull rose higher and higher until we couldn't see its fangs or its teeth anymore.

Only eyes.

On impulse, I reached out and squeezed Kayla back.

"Ow!" Stetler yelped. "Who was that?"

Oops. I drew my hand away. I didn't dare say a word. Especially since the *Creeposaurus rex* skull was MOVING.

Its eerie eye lights rushed down at us like diving birds.

THUMP! The skull crashed to the floor and lay still. Everyone gasped and leapt backward.

Was it killed? Was it broken?

Of course not. A long neck of intricate, dirt-colored vertebra scraped the floor like a snake, driving the giant skull forward. The jaws opened over our heads.

This is the end, I realized.

Kayla, Darius, Stetler and I huddled up even tighter. Kayla gripped my arm like a vice. Or maybe Stetler did. We were all intertwined, all shaking to the same awful beat.

Death. Would it hurt? Would we feel it?

I didn't know. But in that moment, I remember telling myself, *At least I won't die alone. At least I'm with them. My...my friends.*

A shadow fell over our faces. Bones scraped and connected, and a thick gob of slime hit my cheek as the air chilled and the temperature dropped below freezing.

I couldn't bear the suspense anymore. I shut my eyes. Seconds later, I felt the first tooth as it pushed through my skin, like the tip of a spear. Then—

"STOP!" cried a voice.

I opened my eyes to the rumble of footsteps.

Clomp. Clomp. Clomp.

The suit of armor clanked into view.

40.

IT HAPPENED IN THE BLINK OF AN EYE. The deadly pressure on my skin vanished as the *Creeposaurus rex* drew away. Its huge body teetered over our heads—

And collapsed.

"Waaah!?" shouted everyone.

Bones from its huge body rained from the sky. Kayla, Darius, Stetler and I rushed around, dodging bones the size of golf carts.

CLUNK! CLUNK! CLUNK!

Huge objects pelted the floor. It was like being caught in a hailstorm. No. A meteor shower.

My ears screeched with sound. With all the crashes, I thought for sure we were dead. It was a miracle we hadn't been hit yet.

Or was it?

I glanced at the suit of armor. Light blazed from its visor. Its metal arms were outstretched, almost scarecrow-like. And then suddenly—

CLAAAANG!

Its heavy gloves smashed together. There was a wild ringing sound. Sparks sprayed the air, casting even more light, as bones jerked to a stop in mid-plunge. A piece of

Creep jaw that was inches from crushing me swerved to the side, drifting weightlessly to the ground, like a feather.

A long moment passed. Then, suddenly, every bone on the ground sprang alive. There were loud slurps and clicks as the bones swarmed together with dizzying speed. In the space of a gasp, they formed buildings. No. Towers! No. Ziggurats!

Wait. Is ziggurat even a word?

The scale of transformation was shocking. Any doubts about who was inside the suit of armor were squashed, emphatically, by its awesome power in shaping the bones.

"It's him," Kayla whispered.

"The Sorcerer," I said, awestruck.

More and more buildings sprang up. The outer walls swirled with color. I saw green-gray with flashes of red. Muddy brown with white lumps. Even eye-melting yellow. All the colors of fossiliferous rock, smushed together.

"It's…a city," said Stetler.

Darius slowly lifted his cell phone.

And then, just as quick as it started—

"AAAARRRRGGGGH!" wailed the voice in the armor. "NOT AAGAAIN!"

The city of fossils collapsed.

It was like an invisible Godzilla attacking. All the domes and towers tumbled back into bones, forming huge clumps on the floor.

The Sorcerer turned to us.

"YOU!" he cried. "YOU AND YOU!"

His heavy arms pointed at Kayla and me.

Wait. No, they didn't.

"Me?" squeaked Darius.

"ME?" Stetler wailed, just as rat-like.

The Sorcerer waved his metal glove. One of the bone piles stirred. Seconds later, a pair of middleweight Creeps *exploded* out of it, dashed forward, and used their jaws to seize Darius and Stetler around the waist, dragging them off toward the pulsing, silver-red light in the distance.

My mouth fell open. Darth Vader's force throw couldn't have pulled them away any faster.

"W-Where are you taking them?" I cried.

The Sorcerer didn't speak. He turned his back on Kayla and me, striding after the Creeps and their prey.

Clomp. Clomp. Clomp.

"Nooo!" Kayla wailed. And as I stood there, trembling and glued to the floor, Kayla balled her fists up and CHARGED.

She made it four or five steps. Then, without looking back, the Sorcerer flung out a hand.

WHOOOSH! Bones flew from every direction.

I let out a scream. "KAYLA!"

I rushed forward, not even thinking—just in time to be trapped by the same ghoulish, gray ribs that formed a cage around Kayla.

Yes. A rib cage.

We watched, helpless, as the Sorcerer's huge body merged with the silver-red light.

He was gone.

41

I SLUMPED AGAINST THE BARS of the rib cage, all the strength draining out of my limbs. I felt numb. Weightless.

Useless.

I'd just watched my friends being dragged away by bone zombies. (Okay, one friend and one Stetler). And at the critical moment, when they *needed* me, where was the great Dr. Arlo Vreeland? Trembling in a corner. Hoping the Creeps wouldn't come for him, too.

I wasn't a hero. I didn't belong in the same zip code as heroes. I didn't even belong on their PLANET.

"Useless!" cried a voice. "I can't get *anything* right!"

I nodded along, thinking I must be delirious. My own thoughts were being shouted out loud. Then I turned and saw Kayla. She was pounding her head on the bars.

"AAARRRGGGHH! I—MESSED—UP—AGAIN!" She grabbed her silvery hair in both fists. "SUPPOSED— TO—BE—DIFFERENT!" Tufts of hair drifted out of her hat brim and sank to the floor. She toppled down, too.

"Different?" I said. "Different how?" Then my brain jolted. "Oh, right. I forgot you've been here before. In the Tomb."

"So have you." Kayla's words were a whisper.

I let her stew for a while. Then I said carefully, "What really happened at the dig site that morning? I saw the pictures. All I remember is tripping and falling into that—"

"No," Kayla interrupted. "You didn't fall."

"I...I didn't'?"

Kayla took a deep breath. "We were playing," she said, "near the warning flags. It was my idea. I thought the Sorcerer's Tomb must be down in that chasm. It was too deep and narrow for adults to explore. I only wanted a peek. But...I tripped. I fell in."

"Wait? *You* fell in? But then how did I—?"

"How did you end up in the chasm?" Kayla finished my sentence. "That's easy. You jumped."

My heart shook. My skin prickled. My eyes popped! I don't know what I expected to hear, but not THAT.

"I...I...no I didn't!" I spluttered.

"You did, Arlo. It was the bravest thing I've ever seen. You watched me fall in the chasm and you didn't think twice. You dove after me." Kayla sighed. "Of course, if you'd have stopped to look, you might've seen the safety rope I was clinging to. I...didn't fall down all the way.

"But *you* did. I felt the wind on my face as you whooshed past me. *You* were the first person to reach the bottom of the chasm. *You* discovered...this place."

My heart raced. "The Sorcerer's Tomb," I whispered.

"I used the rope to climb after you," said Kayla, "but by then it was too late. You'd already gotten the full blast of...*Umklasum*. The curse. Well, we both did."

"The Bone Gate," I murmured. "Lend your bones."

"The Heart Gate," Kayla replied. "Lend your heart."

My heart jolted. "W-Whaaat?"

Kayla clutched her silvery hair, looking grim. "It started the day after we got back. At first, it was just this weird, hollow feeling. Then my hair changed from red to gray, like it was dying or something, and I started dreaming about the message glowing on the wall when we opened the archway. *Lend your heart*. Finally I realized what happened. The Sorcerer's Tomb took my heart."

"No!" I gasped.

Kayla nodded. "Even now I can sense it: the hole in my chest. I don't look or feel normal. My hair grows too fast, and it always turns gray and falls out."

"I like your hair," I mumbled.

"And it's getting worse," Kayla went on. "The hollow feeling makes it harder to sleep, harder to study. My straight-A's are slipping. And obviously no one wants to hang out with me. They think I'm this big, weirdo freak."

"Don't be crazy," I said. "Everyone loves you! Okay, so you sit alone at the lunch table. But that's only because you're, uh, *you*. You're pretty and smart and put-together and, uh…it's kind of intimidating, actually." I swallowed.

"Oh, whatever," said Kayla.

"It's true! I've been trying for *weeks* to find the nerve to talk to you. Every time I got close, I wimped out. And then Stetler came along…"

My cheeks reddened. I felt a flush of embarrassment.

To my astonishment, Kayla flushed too.

"My mom's doing," she muttered. "She thought I needed a friend. She set the whole thing up, actually."

"And she chose...Stetler?" I marveled. *"Craig Stetler?"*

"Well, no. She chose you, actually." Kayla flushed again. "Mom never understood why we stopped hanging out. But I knew I couldn't face you. I know what the Sorcerer cost you, Arlo. What *I* cost you."

"Kayla..."

She waved me away.

"Craig Stetler isn't that bad. Our families play tennis together. He's a little clingy, I guess, but it's nice having someone to talk to. He's helping me cope. And I think I'm helping him, too. He's got a lot of anger built up, but he's making progress."

I almost laughed out loud. "Stetler punches my arm just for *looking* at him!"

"He doesn't mean to," Kayla insisted.

I snorted.

"Besides," she said, "he's been a big help with the mission. When I heard a museum was being built on top of our dig site, I knew I had to see it, just on the off chance I could do something. Fix something.

"Then, a few weeks ago, I learned about our class trip. It was the perfect excuse. I could find the Tomb again. I could smash that awful red rock inside, once and for all."

Kayla snaked an arm through the rib cage, pointing at the silver-red light in the distance.

"That rock is what's hurting us, Arlo. You've seen those bone creatures' eyes. The red light. It's the source of the curse! I know it." She balled her fists. "Argh! If I could just get close to it! I'd do a lot more than chip a piece off the top." Kayla smiled savagely.

"You're talking about the bauxite," I said. "The charms on our necklaces."

Kayla's eyes flicked from me to the open Tomb door. "Guess you still wear yours, huh?"

"You too," I replied. "But…why didn't you tell me this sooner? I could've helped you. I would've!"

Kayla shook her head. "You've suffered enough because of me. That's why I tried to get you stuck at school today. I wanted you safe. I kept thinking, what if you lost more bones? What if you died?"

"What if *you* die?" I snapped. "In case you forgot, the Sorcerer brought us here. Whoever he is, he sent out bone invitations. He knew about our trip all along. How do you explain *that?*"

"I…I had to try something!" Kayla protested. "But typical me, I just screwed it all up. We can't do a thing from this cage. Now *you're* trapped here. And Craig, too. And Darius. I've doomed everyone."

She gave a muffled sob.

My jaw fell open. I tried to say something useful (I still don't know what) but all at once, Kayla's expression shifted. Her eyes shrank and her lips tightened into a line. She drew a steel chisel out of her pocket and started whaling on the bars of the rib cage, trying to blast them apart.

Nothing happened.

She still didn't stop.

"I'm getting us out of here," Kayla vowed. "I have to. I *will.*"

CLINK! Her chisel crashed down on the ribs. And again. And again.

I watched with bated breath. My thoughts raced. I knew we had to get out of the rib cage. But I also knew, then, who the least-qualified person to lead a daring escape was.

Me.

I mean, wasn't it obvious? Kayla was a billion times tougher than me. Stetler was faster and stronger. Darius was crazy, which meant he could probably do anything. So why was I the one who could easily slip out of the rib cage whenever I wanted?

Yes.

I hadn't told Kayla about my ability. I let her go on and on, sharing stories and stabbing her chisel. We even laughed a few times. The smell of our sweat mixed with Pearberry body spray.

I loved it. It almost felt like old times.

But it wasn't heroic. Not even close.

Five minutes passed. Ten minutes. Kayla was still focused, still chipping away at the ribs, despite the fact she'd barely put a scratch in one. There was a wild gleam in her eye. The vein in her neck pulsed insanely.

That's when I realized she wasn't going to stop. She'd keep swinging until either the rib snapped or she fainted and died.

Now tell me that isn't heroic.

But her heart, I thought crazily. *Kayla's missing her heart!*

Was she, though? I found it hard to believe. Losing bones I understood. After all, there was plenty of evidence. But a heart? A human heart?

I thought back to the Creeps. All those eerie red eyes. Could the Creeps be using Kayla's heart as a power source? Maybe the red rock Kayla mentioned was evil. And the Sorcerer, too.

Clink. Clink. Clink.

Kayla chipped away at the ribs. She barely spoke anymore. Her chest heaved and her arms moved like rotors.

She looked desperate. Determined. Ferocious.

Did I have one-tenth of Kayla's courage?

No. And I probably never would, ever.

All I had was…the one thing we desperately needed. A way to escape. Even if I was the worst guy for the job. Even if bone zombies would probably catch me before I'd taken two steps.

Kayla needed me. *Kayla Caine.*

How could I sit around and do nothing?

I suddenly balled up my fists. "I'll…I'll do it!" I blurted out. "I'll smash the evil red rock. I'll make the Sorcerer pay for what he did to you!"

And then, almost without thinking, as if I'd always intended it, I slipped through the bars.

42

KAYLA STARED IN AMAZEMENT. The two ribs I'd squeezed through were about an inch apart. Maybe less. From across the bars, I watched the gears in her head spinning. Her mouth slowly opened and closed.

"Your bones," she said softly. "Of course…"

Then her dark eyebrows scrunched.

"You idiot, Arlo! You should've TOLD ME you could do that!"

"Look who's talking," I said.

But on the inside, I was totally freaking out. I knew there was no turning back. Not after revealing my secret ability.

The cat was out of the bag. The freak was out of the fossilized rib cage, whether he liked it or not.

And the hero is staying behind, I thought grimly.

Kayla slapped the bars uselessly. She was still trapped in the ribs. Nothing I did could change that. There was no key I could steal to unlock them. No magic tool I could swing.

I just had to win. That was all.

To defeat the Sorcerer. To smash the evil red rock.

An icy chill bled down my neck. The enormity of the task ahead—facing the Sorcerer alone, without any real plan, without *backup*—had finally sunk in, like a cold-water bath.

I turned to go. Because what else could I do?

"Arlo, wait! Don't be stupid!"

I spun around. "It's fine, Kayla, I'm not being—*OOF!*"

My vision went gray. I felt a funny twinge on my head. A second later, I raised the cowboy hat that was blocking my eyes.

"For luck," Kayla said, grinning.

Her other hand snaked through the bars. A cold weight settled into my palm.

"For revenge," she whispered. "For us."

I looked down at my palm. Kayla had passed me her chisel.

"Destroy it," she hissed. *"Kill the rock."*

Her fingers closed around mine. A long moment passed. I don't know how to explain it, except that all the strength in my body got pulled toward my eyes. Kayla and I shared a look.

Do you know how long it had been since that happened? As kids, we used to hang out all the time. But as middle-schoolers, Kayla treated me like a bug with too many legs. She left the room when I entered. She never looked me in the eye for more than a second.

Until now.

Forget about the Sorcerer. Forget EVERYTHING.

I could've stood there forever. I *would've*. But—

BOOOOOM!!!

The entire Tomb started shaking. There were distant squeaks, like a pair of rats singing mezzo-soprano.

"AAAaaaahhh!"

"AAAAaaaaahhhhh!"

"Go!" shouted Kayla. "Go! Go!"

She jerked her head toward the silver-red light. I stared at it. Whatever was going down, it was going down there.

On the dance floor.

Ugh. Why did I keep thinking that?

As I turned to leave, I stole a glance at the Tomb's open door. A large fossil was wedged in the gap, holding it open.

My thoughts raced. At first, I wondered if the Sorcerer had put the fossil there on purpose. But why would he do that?

Then my heart jolted. *I could run,* I realized. *The Sorcerer isn't watching. He can't stop me leaving.*

It happened so quickly. A split-second.

I raced to the door.

"Arlo!" Kayla shrieked. "WHAT THE HECK ARE YOU DOING?"

I didn't stop to explain.

I reached the door at a jog. A part of me really did want to run. However, a better part of me—not necessarily a bigger part—squished to a halt behind the empty Heart Gate. I reached down and scooped a pair of necklaces off the ground, where they'd fallen after being fed through the slot.

Maybe I was still in a daze after talking to Kayla. Maybe I'd seen too many Harrison Ford movies. But I couldn't leave them. Not once I spotted their glow.

You're probably wondering why I cared about my necklace at all. Why did I still wear it after so many years?

I don't know. I guess it made me feel good inside. It reminded me of a time I was happy. When I wasn't a freak. When I had friends, and all my bones were intact.

Maybe Kayla felt the same way. Maybe that's why she still wore hers, too.

But that's not the only reason I grabbed the necklaces. Basically, I realized the red rocks had power. They'd allowed the Tomb door to open. They were connected to the Creeps and the Sorcerer.

They *mattered*. If not to the mission, then to me. To us.

Kayla was scowling as I trotted back to the rib cage. "Almost gave me a heart attack," she gasped. "Arlo, what on Earth were you—"

"Here," I interrupted, all suave-like. "For luck!"

Half out of breath from jogging, I reared back and sent her charm necklace sailing through the bars of the cage.

Really.

At least that was my plan. What actually happened was, my shoulder slipped from its socket. The necklace I meant to throw ended up whacking me across the forehead.

"Ow!" I yelped.

The chain slid down my neck and intertwined with the second one, which I was already wearing.

It formed a knot. A huge knot.

Kayla shook her head in amazement. "You idiot," she mouthed. When I tried to protest, she just jerked her head sideways. "Go, Arlo! GO!"

So I went.

LIKE THEY SAY IN old movies, it was quiet; too quiet.

My shoes scuffed the floor as I walked. I heard my own shaking breath. My own heartbeat.

I peered around. Any second, I expected the Creeps to jump out and attack me. I didn't understand why they HADN'T.

Where were the bones? What caused the rumbles and squeaks I'd heard earlier?

What was lurking in the silver-red light?

As I moved closer, the cowboy hat drooped down my face. I kept adjusting the band, but it still wouldn't sit right. I wondered if Kayla had broken it somehow. Or maybe the hat liked her best.

Either way, it did nothing to calm my nerves. Maybe Dr. Arlo Vreeland could feel brave in a fake plastic hat, but not me. Not Arlo the Freak.

"Unngh!"

I groaned as the cowboy hat slid down my eyes again. I drew a sharp breath through the plastic. Pearberry body spray flooded my nostrils.

My thoughts swirled. My heart fluttered.

And I stopped thinking so much about hats.

About a minute later, feeling oddly refreshed, but still panicked, a burst of silver-red light stung my eyes.

The evil red rock.

There it was.

43

THE FIRST THING I SAW were the coffins. There were two of them, arranged side by side on a raised platform pulsing with light. They looked like Egyptian sarcophagi, only bigger and plainer. They were also... *carved out of bone.*

My skin prickled. I inched closer, trying to calm my beating heart. The scariest thing was the silence. I glanced around. Nothing creaked. Nothing moved.

I took a deep breath. Where was the Sorcerer?

Where was anyone?

Doesn't matter, I thought. *You've got work to do.*

I raised a leg and rolled myself onto the platform. Silver light pulsed from the coffins. Leaning close, I saw a long line of pictograms. There was no English this time. No cobwebs or dust, either. The coffin lids shimmered like ice.

Between the coffins were two objects. The first was smooth and flat like a corkboard. It had pins in it, and random objects that drooped down the side like a Christmas tree.

The second—you guessed it—was the evil red rock. It sat on an old pedestal streaked with dust and dirt. A layer of grime coated the rock's surface, too, as if it hadn't been polished in years.

Of course, that didn't dull the light blazing off it.

"Unnngh," I moaned, shielding my eyes.

I had to squint to keep my head from exploding. Even then, I couldn't look long. I kept turning away and turning back again.

I felt sickened by the rock, but also mesmerized. Its strange shape was burned across my eyelids. The way it pulsed and throbbed, like a living thing.

"Kayla never said what it looked like…" I murmured.

I drew a slow, shaky breath.

Yes. The evil red rock was a heart.

Thump-thump. Thump-thump.

I almost screamed as the sound filled my ears. It was a low pulse, like a drum. I felt an icy hand seize my chest. It started squeezing me. Prying my ribs apart.

OH MY GOD, I thought. *OH MY GOD.* I staggered back, clutching my chest. *No…please…you can't take it…*

It was a moment before I realized the pressure and sound came from me. My heart was beating out of control. The evil red rock hadn't thumped. It was me. My own fear.

Half-gasping, I glanced at the coffins. Every hair on my neck stood on end.

If the red rock was alive…then what was hiding inside of the coffins? A living thing? A true zombie?

Silver light stung my eyes as I stared. I held my breath, waiting for something to happen. Would the lids twitch? Would they rumble and squeak?

What was in them?

My legs quivered. I suddenly felt like an intruder. A trespasser. I felt an intense sense of wrongness.

"I shouldn't be here," I muttered. "I *really* shouldn't be here." I pulled my hat down my face and breathed deeply.

Focus, I told myself. *You have a job to do. Kayla needs you.*

Still trembling, I pulled the chisel out of my pocket and turned to the rock. Eerie light splashed my arm as I raised it over my head.

I heard the sound again. *Thump-thump. Thump-thump.*

"Ignore it, ignore it," I mumbled.

I stared at the rock. There was a small chink in its surface, near the top of the heart. *Kayla's mark.*

A web of cracks showed the spot where Kayla's chisel had struck seven years ago. I decided to aim for it, to maximize damage.

My jaw clenched. My hand squeezed the chisel.

I froze.

Something didn't feel right. Could I really do this? *Should* I do this?

My thoughts rambled. Why did the evil red rock have to be heart-shaped? And why did it PULSE? Why did it feel so…ALIVE?

I hate killing things. I don't know why. It's against my DNA. Exploding a rock is all right. But destroying a *heart?*

I drew in a breath. But if that's what it took to save Kayla…to save my friends from the Creeps…to save *me*…

Yes. If Kayla's hunch was correct, then by destroying the rock, I could do more than win her heart back.

I could take back my bones.

With a full skeleton, I could run and jump again. I could pour Dad's freaky bone syrups down the drain, and I'd never have to see another doctor's shocked face during checkups. I wouldn't be picked on at school, or not picked at all during gym class. I wouldn't be Arlo the Freak.

It was everything I'd ever wanted. And all it would take was one swing. The chisel would pierce the chink in the rock. It would finish the job Kayla started.

One swing. Okay, maybe two or three swings. Or four. However many it took, it was doable. It was *easy*.

So how come I felt so revolted?

A fresh wave of wrongness swept through me. I tried to force it away. To ignore it.

Being a hero means being brave, I told myself. *Maybe it's supposed to feel wrong. Maybe that's why it's tough.*

I thought about all those movies and TV shows where the lead actors can't fall asleep. They lie awake at night, dreaming of terror and death. They can never escape their dark past.

Was that in my future? Was that the cost of becoming a hero? Did heroes do things as crazy as killing a heart?

I clenched my teeth, trying to summon more strength.

"Doing!" urged a voice. "Doing now!"

My eyes widened. Once again I had that delirious feeling of someone speaking my brainwaves out loud.

Clomp. Clomp. Clomp.

Heavy footsteps clambered onto the platform.

My mind froze. The Sorcerer!

44

"HURRIED!" URGED THE VOICE. "Be whamming it quick. Really whacking!"

I spun around.

"I waaaiting," the Sorcerer said through his armor. "Be hurry and breaking it, slowpoke. C'moooonn!"

"Y-You," I sputtered. "Y-You're actually…and you want me to…?"

My voice trailed away. Standing before me was a seven-foot-tall suit of armor. The same terrifying figure who had dragged me through the museum's glass doors.

The one whose boot smashed my chest. The one Uncle Leo had winked at. *The Sorcerer.*

So how come his voice was so shrill and high-pitched? No way could an adult have a voice like that. No way.

The strange voice sent chills down my back. My knees pulsed. My teeth thumped.

"How old are you?" I blurted out.

The Sorcerer's iron head tilted. "More than hundreds and millions! But I also being five and a half. Nopes! Twelve! I forget I grow big ever since I wake up. I wishing I never wake up. Is so…BORING!"

The words were barely out of his helmet when—

BOOOOOM! He tipped backwards and crashed to the floor, shouting, "Unggghh!" in a burst of annoyance.

My chest stiffened. I'd never seen anything weirder.

Then, before I could blink, the Sorcerer raised his arms in the air and squeaked, *"Rise!"*

The stone floor erupted as a dozen earthquakes seemed to strike out at once. Creeps scurried out of the shadows and raced up the platform, surrounding the Sorcerer and lifting his suit back to standing. They rose on tiptoes, making "Kweek!" sounds and prodding their skulls at him.

"Good bones!" said the Sorcerer, petting them. He caught me staring and laughed. "My powers no bad, okay? But comparing Mummy and Daddy, I worse. Is because I defective."

"You're...a detective?" I stared in amazement.

"DEFECTIVE!" The Sorcerer stamped his boot angrily. The Creeps stamped their bony feet, too, casting eerie red glares in my direction.

I felt a sick sense of dread. *This kid is insane,* I thought. *One second he's laughing, and the next he's threatening to kill me!*

My fingers squeezed Kayla's chisel. Could I smash the evil red rock before the Sorcerer sent his Creeps after me? But what if I failed? What if the Creeps got me first?

Silence stretched. Besides the Creeps' clicking teeth, there was a distant clang that made my skin prickle.

CLANG! CLANG! CLANG!

It seemed to ring on a loop through the darkness. What was causing it? Another Creep? Something worse?

My stomach twisted. I realized if I didn't say something soon, I might explode out of fright.

"W-What's your name?" I asked the Sorcerer finally.

A gurgling sound rose from his helmet. I asked him to repeat that, please—and he did. I was really confused.

"S-Santa Claus?" I translated. "King Opossum?"

Then my eyes lit up.

"Wait! Umklasum! Your name is…Umklasum!"

"Umklasum Fourth!" said the Sorcerer. "Daddy third, but Mummy do most, so she first. This what *I* think."

I watched the Creeps as they nodded along with their boss. It was…weird.

Almost as weird as being a kid named *Umklasum*.

"How about I just call you…Klaus?" I said warily.

The Sorcerer hesitated. His army of Creeps, however, grew increasingly stressed. Pointed claws sliced the air.

Uh oh, I thought. Had I pushed it too far?

"Klaus…Klaus," mused the Sorcerer. "Oh yes, I loving clawses!"

"Yeah, clearly—"

"You want seeing?"

Suddenly the Sorcerer—Klaus—swung his arm at me.

"ATTACK!" he cried. "GETTING 'IM! GETTING!"

What if I told you the Creeps spun around like a twelve-headed skeleton? Bared their fangs at me? Sprang for my head?

"Aaaaaahhhhhh!" I shrieked. "AAAAaaaaaAAAaahh!"

A rocky claw slashed an inch from my face.

"STOP!" said Klaus. "STOPPING!"

A dozen skeletons froze in mid-jump. They hung for a moment, then smashed to the floor, bursting on impact.

"You AFRAID!" Klaus wailed. "I thinking you different, but no, you is scaring! Same as bad peoples!"

BOOOOOM! His iron suit tipped to the floor again. This time, he kicked his legs in the air like an upside-down turtle. He was totally freaking out.

"PEOPLES AFRAID! They hating castle! Hating bones! Hating me! Is because I defective, DEFECTIVE, DE-FECT-IVEEE!"

His howls sent a fresh group of Creeps rushing in.

"Kweek?!" they wailed. "Kweek?!"

They seemed extremely upset. Bones clinking, they formed a ring around Klaus in his armor. Silver light from the coffins joined the piercing red glow of their eyes.

Guess what else? All those eyes suddenly focused on ME. "Uh…uh…uh…" I said, stumbling backward.

The Creeps advanced in a wave. Though small, they moved like demon dogs—the zombie descendants of Fluffkins.

Panicked, I swung the chisel in my hand like a dagger. Except I didn't know how to swing a dagger.

CLUNK! The chisel slipped from my grasp.

I let out a moan. My jaw clenched as I clutched at my hat, heart and necklaces.

"It's just Fluffkins," I babbled. "Just a dog…little dog…twenty dogs…"

I uttered a gasp as the first Creep swung its claw at me. These 'little dogs' were about to rip me apart!

45

I WAS ABOUT TO DIE. Clearly. So it's not surprising I saw my life flash before my eyes. All my mistakes. All my uselessness.

Why did it have to be me?

Why was *I* the one facing Klaus and the Creeps?

If it were Kayla, she would've destroyed the evil red rock already. She wouldn't have waited. No way.

Against Stetler, the Creeps would've been blasted apart in one punch. Even Darius could've swept a few legs for the movie.

Not me.

I was frozen in fear. Trying to pretend these Mini Creep demon dogs didn't want a pound of my flesh for a snack.

I started hallucinating.

Dogs. Maybe they really were dogs. Only dogs.

"Shoo!" I begged. "Scram! Go away!"

When that failed, I used my inner thesaurus.

"Back away! Discontinue! Bad doggy!"

WHOOOSH! My arm hairs shook as a lunging claw forced me back to the edge of the platform. I was running out of time. Out of real estate. The lead Creep was rearing back for a jump.

I inhaled a breath—likely my last breath on Earth—and cried, "Heel! HEEL!"

I don't know what stupid power possessed me.

Flashbacks of *Paw Patrol? The Dog Whisperer?*

All I know is the evil red rock surged with power. Light blazed from my tangled-up necklaces, and a shiver fell over the Creeps. They didn't freeze in mid-air, but they stopped. They stood still at my side.

"Kweek?" they whined. "Kweek? Kweek?"

"S-Sit," I commanded. They sat.

"L-L-Lay down," I said, stupefied—and the Creeps all laid down.

But not Klaus. He staggered to sitting position. I felt his invisible eyes rake across me. Then he leapt to his feet.

"I KNOWING you different! I KNOWING!"

My ribs squished as Klaus pulled me into a hug.

"You have powers!" he said excitedly. "I was thinking you MIGHT, but not knowing for sure!"

"Oww," I gasped. "Owww. Owww."

When I finally stopped wheezing, Klaus led me through a series of exercises. He taught me to focus my will on the evil red rock—the *Umdadum*, he called it. I learned to issue commands using short bursts of energy.

Brainwaves, I guess. Focused thoughts.

To demonstrate, he dismantled the Creeps with a wave of his arm. "Now you trying!" he chirped. "Making more!"

So I did. Half-delirious, as if I were lost in a dream, or maybe the afterlife, I mustered all of my strength. Focused hard. Shrank my will until it resembled the tip of an arrow.

And…spoke.

"Rise!" I boomed. *"Rise!"*

The *Umdadum* pulsed with excitement. It flopped around on its pedestal. It squished and slurped like a living thing. Like a real human heart.

My chest throbbed where the necklaces hung in a knot.

"Rise!" I repeated. *"Rise! Rise!"*

On my tenth try, I successfully sent a bone whizzing into my hand. Except I fumbled the catch and got conked in the head.

"Yeooww!" I cried.

The other bones flopped away from me.

"They shy," said Klaus. "They sensing your big power!"

"My big…power?"

"Very big!" Klaus assured me. Then he paused for a moment. "Bigger," he said softly. "No. *Biggest.*"

And he didn't speak for a while.

My head was throbbing with pain. Either the flying bone left a dent in my skull, or I was slowly regaining my senses. Maybe both.

I rubbed my eyes, blinking back to reality.

I was inside the Sorcerer's Tomb. Not only that, I was controlling the bones. Zombie bones!

I felt a stab of horror that sharpened the longer I stood there. What just happened? What the heck was I DOING?

Where was Kayla? Where were Stetler and Darius?

Nerves shaking, I turned to Klaus in his huge suit of armor. I needed answers and I needed them now.

I opened my mouth—but words failed me. My voice came out hoarse and cracked and, in the end, all I managed was, "H-H-H-How?"

Klaus's iron suit creaked as he looked me over.

"You no remember? Okay, fine. I tell story!"

THUMP!

His iron gloves came together. Suddenly bones wriggled out of their piles and stitched themselves into armchairs. Klaus whooped and sat down while the other chair bumped my legs from behind. I tumbled into it, gasping.

And Klaus started his story.

"MANY, MANY YEARS AGO," Klaus began, "Mummy and Daddy are building Tomb of Umklasum, for when we no longer living. But old peoples wicked. Mummy and Daddy die quick. MUCH UPSET. I go to hide in Tomb, too. I seal myself up but no die, because…because of…"

Klaus searched for a word.

"Cold freezing? Ice age?"

I blinked. "You can't mean…*cryogenically frozen?*"

"I NO CRY!" Klaus shrieked.

The bones in our armchairs clicked loudly.

"Whoa!" I cried. "Fine! You don't cry, you don't cry!"

"I no cry," Klaus agreed. He inhaled a breath, slapping his mask where a pale droplet leaked down the seam.

I pretended not to notice.

"While in Tomb," Klaus went on, "I no age and no die for much time…UNTIL SEVEN YEARS AGO. Then I wake unexpected! Alarms singing. Friends have entering Tomb!"

My heart jolted. *Me and Kayla,* I realized.

"But friends is leaving so quick, like a lightning, and afterward Tomb seal up tight. I is trapped. No escape. MANY YEARS. Is okay though! I digging hole. Tiny crack. But enough!"

There was a low creak. I thought Klaus must have puffed out his chestplate. He seemed pretty proud of escaping.

"In outside world, I seek friends. VERY HARD. Is like alien planet! But I have super plan: to rebuild holy city of bones. Every building so good and so high!

"Except…I cannot. No have big magic like Mummy or Daddy. *Umdadum* no bless me like you. As I saying, I weak. I…defective!"

The bones in our chairs stirred uneasily. I felt a spike of alarm. No. A spike of BONE. ("Oww!")

I willed the bone to stop pricking my armpit—and it *did,* finally—then gave Klaus a nod of encouragement.

"It's okay," I said. "What happened next?"

Klaus sniffed. "Next I building this place. Museum. I use gold treasure and many big bones. Simple shapes— like your big holy castle! But I young still, and peoples no believe I am boss. They no trust. So I hide in big iron suit. Hide my body. Protect me."

"You put on a costume," I murmured.

"Exactly!" said Klaus through his helmet. "Wearing suit I am big peoples boss. Except bad, because peoples afraid. Still no help. Is why I hire friend Leo. Leo no scream when I walk or talk or do bone switch. He no paying attention, I think. But is good!"

My brow furrowed. That sounded like Uncle Leo all right. So it was Klaus who hired him...Is that why Uncle Leo didn't flinch when Klaus dragged me away? Because he recognized Klaus in his armor?

So weird.

Klaus cleared his throat. "Giving gold to friend Leo, he buying interesting things so museum grow big. Attract friends. MUCH IMPORTANT. Friends must find Tomb of Umklasum. I adding signs. I write English on wall. Is it help? Are you seeing?"

"The Sorcerer's Tomb," I said. "Yeah, I saw. But why not write 'Tomb of Umklasum?'"

"Sorcerer is MYSTERY word!" Klaus replied. "Much excite! Like in holy book one!"

Holy book one? I thought, baffled.

"I also writing subtext," said Klaus, plunging on. "Only the Panicked Shall Pass. You have seeing? I saying this every day I is scared. *Do not shake. Do not sobbing. Your panicked shall pass. Friend will come.* This words helping me calm, so maybe it helping more peoples nervouses."

I felt a lump in my throat.

"But friend no come easy. I try more. I leaving castle and suit to find teachings. I fixing old bones, building ultimate creature. BEST CREATURE. Every bone that is good! But peoples still hate. No liking this new bones AT ALL."

Klaus slumped in his chair, causing more bones to quake. The air shivered dangerously.

"I...I like them!" I blurted out.

"You...like?" Klaus perked up.

"Y-Yes," I said frantically. "The *Creeposaurus rex* is my favorite. I love the fangs. The spiked back. The, uh, bone-crusher tail. You combined all the scariest—ahem, all the *best* parts of dinosaurs into one awesome package. My friend and I love it so much, we're actually filming a movie with the *Creeposaurus rex* as the monster."

I beamed at Klaus. I thought his tantrum was over.

It wasn't.

"NO MONSTER!" Klaus wailed. "Creeposaurus PROTECTING. Good creature!"

"Uh, sure! You're right. I mean—"

"IS NO SCARING!" Klaus shrieked even louder. "Only bad peoples scaring. Because bad peoples SHOULD BE!"

His angry voice echoed over the Tomb. There were multiple clicking sounds, rising over the clangs in the distance.

My muscles tensed.

I knew I had to tread carefully. Klaus's personality was like a volcano that could erupt any second. If I got on his bad side, there was no telling what would happen.

No way could I stop all those Creeps from attacking again.

Not to mention what could happen to Kayla.

It was time to leave. Time to make my excuses and very politely ask Klaus to release my friends from whatever dungeons or rib cages they were trapped in.

I'd already failed to destroy the *Umdadum*. I'd had a crisis of faith. I'd wimped out.

Now the only safe move was to flee.

So how come my brain wouldn't listen?

Blood rushed to my head. Something about Klaus's tantrum was bugging me. Grinding my gears.

I felt a burst of annoyance.

In that moment, I didn't care if Klaus's true age was five and a half or twelve or nine hundred million. I didn't even care that he suffered so much.

Because…he deserved it! How dare he act so pathetic in front of me! Seven years ago, he stole Kayla's heart. He took my bones! This sad little freak ruined both of our lives. And for what? He didn't even apologize!

I suddenly balled up my fists.

"Seven years ago," I said quietly—stupidly, desperately—"when my friend and I unlocked the Tomb, you claimed you were happy to see us. But if that's true, then why did you hurt us? Why did you ruin our lives…with the curse of Umklasum?"

Klaus froze in mid-whine. Silver and red lights pulsed across his armor. Their movements grew wilder. Faster.

"CURSING!" Klaus shrieked. "CURSING! You…you daring think…AAAARRRRGGGGH!"

A violent cry burst through his helmet. Klaus lunged forward. The armchair beneath me dissolved and I crashed to the floor.

Staring up at him.

Klaus's iron suit towered over me, as thick as a tombstone. A thousand eyes lit the shadows around us. Light from the *Umdadum* splashed off Klaus's chestplate and into my eyes, flashing angrily. Vengefully.

I cringed in terror—

And saw an iron boot smashing down on me.

46

THERE WAS A MUFFLED SCREAM.

A flash of intense déjà vu. A loud SQUISH!

Then, just as quickly as the boot stomped, it lifted. The pressure on my lungs released. I almost sobbed as I gulped down a breath, feeling my squished bones reforming.

I'd survived. I could breathe!

"You seeing?" said Klaus, energized. "STILL NO DIE. Is big gift from Daddy to you. Is no cursing! So why speaking rubble?"

"R-Rubble?" I gaped at him. "You mean…rubbish?"

"YES! RUBBLISH!"

Klaus waved a glove and the Creeps dragged me onto my feet. I swayed on quivering knees, feeling numb.

"Tomb of Umklasum is VERY GOOD THING," Klaus insisted. "Is no cursing. NO EVER. For friends finding first, many gifts giving!"

"But your Tomb took my bones," I said. "It took my friend Kayla's heart."

"Peoples too many bones," Klaus said dismissively. "Less is leaner. More room for good magic. As for heart thief, I thinking no. You is wrongly believing."

His iron glove tapped his chestplate.

"How is human hearts disappearing? No happen. No unless bad peoples killing. Then yes."

My eyes strayed to the pulsing *Umdadum*.

"No, no!" Klaus shook his head frantically. "*Umdadum* is no peoples heart. Is ancestor gift. Sacred rock!"

I stared at him.

"Okay, wow, I explaining. Be listen, okay?" Klaus cleared his throat. "First time I entering Tomb, Daddy already using big magic, for when I awake after sleep, I no wake alone. In future world, I have brother. Extra peoples with power."

Klaus stretched his arm at me, nodding seriously.

"Mummy also use magic. She is giving most beautiful feature: the Sorceress hair. So in future world, I have wife."

I almost spat out my tongue.

"W-Wife?" I choked. "You mean...Kayla Caine?"

Klaus giggled. "Is okay! I no care about wife. Only bones!"

As he spoke, a line of Creeps flung their bodies together. Their skeletons twisted and slurped until a single large Creep emerged, roaring.

"RAAWWR!"

Its spine arched, almost cat-like, with three rows of murderous spikes. Fangs plunged beneath its curving, carnivorous teeth, and its lower jaw jutted out like a crocodile's snout.

An orthodontist would've fainted from shock.

And that's not even mentioning the cannonball tail sweeping over its head. People complain about Labrador tails. Hah. Try standing next to a Creep.

I took a wary step back.

"You are liking?" Klaus asked. "I designing! Is seventeenth model. I letting him roaming museum today. BIG SURPRISE. Peoples whose asking can hover on back, like on hippo or nimbus. Only…"

Klaus's voice fell to a whisper.

"…no be asking policemen, I think. Much afraid."

I stared at the *Creeposaurus rex* skeleton. My hand slid to my pocket.

"Here," I said, presenting Dad's packet of bone diagrams to Klaus. "These are real dinosaur skeletons. I know the *Creeposaurus rex* is already cool, but these can help you make more things. Things that people won't run away from or laugh at."

"Is…instructions kit?" said Klaus warily.

"Sure," I said. "Like in Cine-Blocks."

"What is…Simba block?"

I shook my head a little. "You know what? Nevermind. You should probably stick with bones, anyway."

"Bones is good!" Klaus agreed. He accepted the packet. "I always wanting improvements. My collection LARGE. I shuffling bones using slippery roads. Skeletons leaner and meaner. Move better. LIKE US!"

Klaus tapped my arm, nodding vigorously.

My eyes drooped.

"Not like me," I mumbled. "I can't move at all sometimes. My bones can't support me. I lost too many." My throat clenched. "You think *you're* defective? Try being me. I'm the real defect." I exhaled a breath. I wasn't mad anymore. Just depressed.

"Good bones want fixing? Is no problem. We fixing!"

My brain jolted. I stared at Klaus, hardly daring to breathe. "You can actually…bring my bones back?"

Klaus made a gagging sound through his armor.

"BLECH! No returning bad bones. Fixing good ones! Best be opening ears, okay? Focused!"

TWO MINUTES. That's how long it took to resolve my life's biggest problem. To end my shame and embarrassment.

THUMP! I leapt off the platform's far edge.

THUMP! I hopped right back up and kept running. I sprinted laps around Klaus and the coffins, my heart soaring, and my bones barely squishing at all.

"Good workings!" Klaus cheered. "Trusting good bones, for when good bones trusting you. Is pure mental! REMEMBER: no is scaring! No afraid! Or else…"

BOOOOM! Klaus tipped to the floor in his armor. Then, laughing, he clinked to his feet, dancing a jig across the silver-red platform.

"Oops!" he said, stumbling into a coffin.

"Aaaaahhh!" gasped a voice from within.

My legs squished and I almost fell over.

"WHAT WAS THAT?" I cried.

"Is nothing!" Klaus squeaked. But I didn't trust his response for some reason. My thoughts raced.

"Your parents," I said slowly. "They can't be...*alive* in those coffins?"

"N-No, silly! How you saying? They bones!"

Switching gears, Klaus stepped past the coffins and reached toward the corkboard-shaped object between them. A mobile art piece? A bulletin board?

I couldn't believe all the objects that were pinned to it, including several large books. Klaus laughed at my squinting expression.

"Is how I know English," he explained. "Reading great holy books one to six. I is finding them EVERYPLACE. All peoples reading. Learning MUCH of new world. You want seeing? Move closer!"

I didn't need to move closer. I knew those covers already. *Harry Potter.*

"You do know it's a seven book series?" I said.

Klaus stiffened. "EH? SEVEN?"

It was my turn to laugh.

For the next minute or so, Klaus and I toured his collection. He was like a pack rat crossed with an Art teacher. Across his corkboard hung pencils and pens. Strips of caution tape. A shard of what looked like a broken police shield. And also...

"Darius's cell phone!" I gasped.

A spidery crack split the screen. Incredibly, its tiny rear light was still on, glowing sharply.

"You liking?" said Klaus. "Phones collecting my favorite! Funny lights. Big reactions!" He paused. "Memories MUCH IMPORTANT. Mummy and Daddy in dreamy lands watching. Knowing I is good here. Future world…is okay, you know? Ah, this remind me!"

Klaus started shaking his wrist. Slowly, the armor slid loose and a long, yellow object flopped out.

"Hard, then soft," he said, grabbing it. "Much delight!"

I watched with wide eyes as he pinned it to his corkboard. "That's…spaghetti," I said. "You found that today! That weird sculpture!"

Klaus turned around. He gave me a deep look. There were creaks as he tightened his gloves into fists.

"I trying spread joy with good sculpting," he growled. "Good artistries. Good Creeposaurus. But NO. Bad peoples breaking. They BREAKING!"

CLUNK! He swung his boot at a coffin.

"No one liking! No one want! No one see Tomb of Umklasum but big bullfrog bullies whose breaking, BREAKING, BRRE-AAK-INNG!"

CLUNK! CLUNK! CLUNK!

Klaus's boots stamped the ground. The *Umdadum* flashed as its pedestal wobbled.

"Klaus, don't!" I cried. "You'll break it!"

"IS GOOD THING! Peoples hate? Peoples whacking and whamming? Is fine. I no wanting live ANYWAY!"

"Klaus, stop! You don't mean that!"

"YES, I DO BE MEANING IT!" Klaus glowered at me. "Even YOU wanting break. I knowing truth in both eyes…and I HELPING! I no needing live. Go to dreamy world. Make museum go BOOOM!"

My heart twisted. *Make museum go BOOOM!*

The museum was built of bones. If the *Umdadum* broke, wouldn't the bones it controlled…fall apart?

"Klaus, listen to me!" I begged. "Please! I was wrong! I don't want to break the stone anymore—"

"THEN I BREAKING!" Klaus's iron fists slammed together. Facing the rock, he raised them over his head like a hammer.

"Nooooo!" I cried, rushing forward. I could block him in time. I had to!

My feet slapped the floor, one then another. They didn't slip or squish like I feared. Because…I *didn't* fear. I put my trust in my bones, and my bones trusted me back.

Confidence. Was it really that easy?

I didn't know. But I STILL wasn't quick enough.

Klaus gave a furious shout ("AAAARRRGGGHH!") as his hammer-fists fell. Eyes wide, stomach clenched, I watched as they swerved past the *Umdadum*, landing flush on the coffins below.

BOOOOOM!

It all happened so fast.

The silver lids blasted open.

And two living people flew out.

47

"M-M-MUMMY!" KLAUS CRIED. "Daddy! I sorry! I sorry!"

A pair of skeletons sprang from the coffins and onto pale, clinking feet. Their bones were perfectly preserved.

Human skeletons.

The sight sent chills down my spine. With all the dino action, I'd forgotten there were more types of—

"AaaaaAAaahh!" squealed a voice.

"AaaaaAAaahh!" cried another.

There were loud clicking sounds as Stetler and Darius extracted themselves from the skeletons hugging them. They spun in circles, screaming and trying to shake off more bones.

"Arlo!" they yelled, spotting me.

A second later, I was drawn into a lung-crushing hug. Would you believe it if I said it was *Stetler* who started it? I felt his thick, fleecy hair brush my neck.

Wait a moment…

"Stetler!" I gasped. "Your…your hair!"

"What are you talking about?" said Darius. "Stetler's bald, he doesn't have any—"

"WAAAAAHHH!" Stetler let out a wail.

Tufts of silver hair flowed down his face like a water-fall. He started flailing his arms, looking less like a shark than a wilting dandelion.

The Sorceress hair, I realized. *From Klaus's mom's skeleton!*

It was several seconds before Stetler slapped himself bald again.

"You okay, dude?" said Darius.

"Yeah," I replied. Except Darius wasn't talking to me. He and Stetler were huddled together, shaking from head to toe as they glowered at Klaus in his armor.

"D-Don't trust him, Arlo. H-He's evil! You saw it!"

"Where's Kayla? We have to find her and—"

Clomp. Clomp. Clomp.

Klaus approached, flanked by two walking skeletons.

"Arlo, get behind me! I'll cover you!"

Fists raised, Stetler leapt out ahead of me.

Stetler did that. Craig Stetler.

Although, to be fair, he seemed equally shocked when I ignored him and marched up to Klaus. I wasn't afraid of him anymore. I asked him what the heck was going on.

"Why did you lock my friends into COFFINS?"

Klaus waved a hand. I tried not to flinch when his parents' skeletons waved, too.

"They LONELY," he said. "Seeing peoples good. Even bad peoples."

"Who are you calling bad peoples?" said Stetler.

Klaus wasn't listening. Linking arms with the skeletons, he led them back to their coffins. The skeletons of Klaus's parents walked freely, even vigorously, but they weren't alive. It was Klaus who controlled them.

"I seeing soon," Klaus promised. "But no as soon as I thinking. For now, I protecting *Umdadum*. So no be worries for sleeping, okay? Loving kissing. Goodnight."

The coffin lids closed with a THUMP! I felt a wave of sadness as Klaus backed away.

"I no cry," he said quietly. Then he tipped to the floor with a BOOOM! that left the silent air trembling. No one spoke. Not a single bone clicked. Even the mysterious clanging had stopped, replaced by a thick, icy stillness.

"What...is he?" Darius said finally.

A boy, I thought. *A lonely and scared little boy.*

"A monster," said Stetler. "A zombie king from the land before time."

Darius frowned. "The land before time? Like...the movie?"

Stetler didn't answer. His eyes had fixed on the pulsing *Umdadum*.

"The evil red rock!" he exclaimed. "That's what Kayla's been looking for. It's why we entered this stinking Tomb in the first place. We have to smash it!"

He pressed forward, cracking his knuckles.

"Don't!" I cried. "You – you can't break his rock!"

"Huh? Don't tell me you're *defending* that freak?"

"He's not a freak," I said. "He's just misunderstood. And...a little unstable."

"Unstable?" Stetler sniffed. "That freak had us HUGGING SKELETONS inside of those coffins."

"Mine didn't lay still," Darius whimpered. "It moved, Arlo. *It hugged back.*" He uttered a gasp. "Oh-God, oh-God, he's standing up again!"

There were clinks, slurps and all sorts of horrible noises. An army of Creeps lifted Klaus to his feet. Silver light shone off his armor. The bones of his Creeps shimmered, too. They scurried between Klaus's legs, casting angry red looks.

Stetler balled his huge fists. "D-Don't come any closer, freak! I'm warning you!"

"YOU A FREAK!" shouted Klaus. "Bad peoples. Breaking!"

The first line of Creeps raised its claws. Stetler snarled.

"Don't!" I cried. "Trust me. Don't break the bones! *Eh, Darius?*"

My jaw dropped. My best friend, the big, screaming coward, the one who feared Stetler the most, had slotted in right beside him.

"We'll hold them off!" Darius yelled. "Arlo, you have to break the rock. It's the only thing that'll stop them!"

I started flailing my arms. "You don't get it! We CAN'T break the—"

CLUNK! BOOOM!

"Kaaaa-Waaaaahhhh!"

The two sides collided. There were clinks, shouts and battle cries. The boys disappeared in a shower of bones.

My mind raced. I knew I had to stop this. But how?

225

I couldn't use my powers. Not with Klaus in command. But what if I ran at Klaus? Could I knock him to the ground? Take him out?

I was still paralyzed, running through crazy scenarios, when something flashed on the edge of my vision.

I spun around. A streak of silver flew by. I saw a girl in ripped sleeves. Sweat dribbled down her flushed face. Her ink-black eyes joined a smudged nose and a thin, curling, near-maniacal smile that was several times more vicious than anything I'd seen on that platform.

My first thought was that a real-life Lara Croft had entered the Tomb. A legendary figure. Stronger and tougher than me and Dr. Yacob combined.

I was wrong, of course.

Seeing me, Kayla pressed a finger to her lips. Her other hand clutched an extremely large, club-like bone.

I knew at once what had happened. Kayla hadn't given up after losing the chisel. No. She'd scrounged around, found a loose bone and turned it into a weapon. She'd started frantically pounding the ribs with it—CLANG! CLANG! CLANG!—until they finally collapsed.

She'd escaped. She hadn't needed me, after all.

Maybe she never did.

I saw her wrist trembling. I knew the icy chill of those bones. How they stung to the touch. And here she was, forcefully gripping one. Lifting it high in the air. Leaning over the pulsing *Umdadum*.

"NOOOO!" shouted Klaus. His arms lifted desperately, about to summon more Creeps. But before he could—

BOOOM!

Stetler and Darius came roaring out of the bone pile. They tackled Klaus simultaneously. A high and low hit. He clunked to the ground beneath his attackers.

Kayla shot me a grin. Her expression was even wilder now. Almost wicked. She swung the bone at the helpless, defenseless *Umdadum,* and for an instant, time seemed to stop. Our future flashed before my eyes.

I saw the *Umdadum* exploding. I saw Kayla, flushed with success, rushing up to me. Hugging me. Then slowly comprehending what had happened. That the Tomb was collapsing.

Killing us. Killing Klaus. Killing everyone.

Blood pounded into my bones.

What did it mean to be a hero? Did it mean fighting bone zombies? Staging a daring escape? Risking your life to save a person you hadn't been friends with since kindergarten?

Or did it mean betraying all that? Betraying everything?

I still don't know the answer. But in that moment, I knew what had to happen.

My voice erupted with confidence. "MINE!"

Kayla uttered a scream. Her arm stiffened as the bone in her hand wriggled loose. It soared through the air like fossilized football.

This time I caught it securely, in flexed, boneless fingers. Because I knew that I would.

"Y-Y-Y-You!" Kayla stared in disbelief.

"I can explain!" I threw up my hands. "Kayla, I'm sorry, but I just saved our—"

"AAAAAARRRGGGHHH!" Kayla rushed forward. She was like a force of nature. A tiny, shrieking tornado. Her angry eyes shrank to knives.

"Kayla, stop! Don't! I'm innocent!"

"AAAARRRLLLLOOO!"

I chucked the bone away. My heart went completely berserk. Same as Kayla! It took all my concentration not to slip and fall as we circled one another, like wolves.

No. Like one wolf and one cheeseburger.

For a split-second, I wondered how many heroes died violent deaths before they could explain themselves properly. Desperate, I flung out my willpower. Bones clicked to life. They reared up and grabbed Kayla's ankles.

"HAAAH!" She tore through them like paper. "You're a monster!" she shrieked. "You even GLOW like one!"

She cast her predator's eyes at my neckline. Eerie red light was blazing out of my chest. Same as Creep eyes. Same as the *Umdadum* I nearly bumped into.

Kayla and I had circled so much, we'd switched places.

"That's why you wanted the necklaces!" Kayla spat. "You *need* them. They're linked to your evil dark magic!"

"Kayla, you're wrong!" I cried. "You're making a big mistake. The rock is innocent! You can't destroy—"

"THAT—THING—STOLE—MY—HEART!"

Like a tiny volcano, Kayla's fury ERUPTED. Head lowered, she ran at me like an angry bull. She was sprinting full-out, trying to smash me and the rock in one hit.

And she would. The living bones couldn't stop her. Even if I dodged her attack, how could the *Umdadum* survive? How could anyone?

Think, Arlo, think.

I wish I could tell you that time froze again. That I racked my brains until I found the miracle move—the ultimate, genius solution that would save me, the *Umdadum* and everyone else from a horrible, horrible death.

So I will. It's why I started this book.

Pay attention!

THE FIRST THING I REALIZED was that the *Umdadum* glowed when either Klaus or I drew on its powers. Light, like rippling red water, flowed down its smooth and gemlike exterior…

Except for in one part.

The chink. The thin web of cracks marking the spot where, seven years ago, Kayla's chisel had carved out the charms for our necklaces.

Could the *Umdadum* have suffered damage that day? Did the crack in its 'heart' make it weaker? More importantly, did Klaus know about the damage? Or, having just woken up, had he assumed the *Umdadum* was working normally, and the damaged object was HIM?

Do you see what I'm getting at?

Klaus wasn't weak. His magic wasn't defective. It was the *Umdadum's* fault. The *Umdadum* we broke!

But what clinched it, for me, were the necklaces. How they glowed when I summoned my magic, but never when Klaus acted. Not once.

In our lesson before, Klaus had mentioned my 'big power.' He seemed sad when he said it. As if he thought his power was weaker. That I was more gifted at magic. Not broken like he was.

Not broken. The words jolted my brain.

Klaus didn't know about my necklaces. He didn't know the *Umdadum* had been split into three separate pieces, and that I, by uniting them, was drawing on the *Umdadum's* full strength.

That meant the *Umdadum* wasn't broken for good.

The damage could still be repaired.

I…I could fix it!

That's your dumbest plan yet, said a voice in my head. *You can't fix a rock, dingbat! Even if you could, it's…absurd! It's worse than one of Darius's movie scripts!*

Are you saying the evil red rock, which is actually heart-shaped, and which actually pulses and throbs like a real human heart, isn't working correctly because it's been…broken?

A BROKEN HEART? That's your genius solution?

It was.

IN A BURST OF WILD ENERGY, I seized the necklaces and shoved their bauxite charms against the pulsing *Umdadum*. Except—

"Unngghh!"

Neither necklace tore off. The bands stiffened around my neck. I started choking and gasping. Stumbling breathlessly. Finally, to stop myself falling, I grabbed the *Umdadum* itself.

Yes. I hugged the *Umdadum*.

(Ridiculous).

There was a burst of blinding red light as the rocks reunited. The bauxite charms merged with the stone, just as simply as merging with water, as shockwaves swept over the platform.

WHOOOOOOSH!

The air trembled. The platform beneath us shook wildly, driving everyone back. Kayla tripped to the floor with a thud no one heard. Klaus was already shouting.

"POWERS!" he cried. "GOOD POWERS!"

His suit swelled with light from the platform. Dazzling streaks of silver and red crossed his chestplate in fossil-like swirls. He was on his feet again, cackling and raising his arms.

"RISE!" he said. "RISE!"

The *Umdadum* pulsed faster and brighter than ever. There were deep rumbling noises as our platform rose toward the ceiling.

And it wasn't alone.

The city was springing up all around us. We saw bone buildings rising like weeds. We saw towers...and ziggurats! Like I said before, the scale of transformation was shocking. Far beyond anything I could ever describe.

We held our breath as the finished bone city lay still. An uneasy quiet came over us. Everyone was thinking the same thing.

Would it hold?

Five seconds passed. Ten seconds. Not a single bone moved. The dazzling bone towers didn't wobble or wilt or collapse. They stayed standing. The only sound in the Tomb came from Klaus.

"F-F-Friends!" he gasped. "Friends...I no crying...no crying..."

He dropped to his knees. His voice dissolved into sobs—which dissolved into choking—coughing—spluttering—

"No...can...breathe..." Klaus gasped.

He raised an iron hand to his face.

And he tore off his helmet.

4.8

NOTE TO READERS: when you have a lot of explaining to do (like A LOT) it helps to have a miraculous bone city to use as your backdrop. It also helps when your mysterious, magical host throws an even more jaw-dropping twist at everyone.

Keeps things in perspective, you know?

Less complaining.

WE STARED AT THE space beneath Klaus's helmet. What was in there? What did crazy Klaus look like? Personally, I was expecting a skull. It just sort of made sense. But would it be a human skull? Dino skull? Something worse?

False alarms all around. It was nothing.

Just a hollow, blank space.

"Oh my God," whispered everyone. But a second later, when Klaus's chestplate popped off, there were gasps.

A twelve-year-old boy clambered out of the suit. The bones he'd been using as stilts fell away. They made clicking sounds as we stood there and watched. I think our eyes nearly popped.

"E-Erik Stotz?"

"The new kid?"

A wide smile bloomed across Erik's face. He was jittery and rocking back and forth on his heels. He looked like a lunatic who'd just escaped the asylum.

"SURPRISING!" he exclaimed. "I go to schools? No one speak! No one like! Turning tables, however! So…how you liking me now?"

We traded thunderstruck looks.

"H-H-How?" muttered everyone.

The boy known as Erik Stotz, a.k.a. Klaus, a.k.a. Umklasum the Fourth, waved a finger. Shards of bone hovered into the air. They moved so fast, I could barely believe it. Having trained with Erik/Klaus previously, I saw the improvement at once. It was like watching a YouTube in triple fast-forward.

The bones quickly formed into pictograms.

"ERIK STOTZ," said the English translation. The letters clicked and transformed. "I AM UMKLASUM."

Darius let out a squeal. "His name! It's an anagram!"

"Huh?" I said. "No, it isn't. It's not even close."

Erik/Klaus shook with laughter. "Spelling no perfect, okay? I copy great holy book. Much important for building big castle!"

"What is he talking about?" Kayla whispered.

234

I looked away. Because how do you answer that?

We were all in a state of confusion. This was not helped by 'Erik Stotz', who decided he preferred the name Klaus, after all, then summoned his entire bone army to demonstrate why.

It took about half an hour before we all caught our breath. Klaus and I took turns explaining the situation, with long interruptions as our platform hovered around the city like an orbiting planet.

"Oh-my-God, oh-my-God," said Darius, madly clicking his cell phone.

When we finally touched down to earth (or at least the ancient stone floor) everyone was in much calmer moods. Klaus has this natural charisma. He's like a toddler who never grew up. One by one, he won everyone over.

"Darius, yo, check me out!" Stetler beamed as he pounded a Mini Creep Klaus had set up for him. Its slimy bones clunked to the floor, only to reform again, slightly taller this time.

"One sec, bro," Darius told him. He stood, mesmerized, in front of Klaus's cell phone collection. "Hey, is this *my* phone? Oh my God, it still works! It's been recording this whole time. Oh-man, oh-man, I wonder which direction the lens was pointing!" He disappeared onto Spielberg planet.

Kayla was definitely the last person to accept our situation. She kept clutching her hair, shooting looks at the pulsing *Umdadum*. Despite all my explaining, I was still afraid she would do something—at least until Klaus taught her the trick of the Sorceress hair.

"Is magic!" he squeaked. "Any shape. Any grow. Any color!"

Kayla eyed him skeptically.

"Use MENTAL! Is good trick. Arlo showing!"

"Me?" I said, stunned.

Klaus nodded fervently. So yeah, that's how Kayla and I spent the next half an hour alone together, talking, laughing and turning her hair every color and length we could think of.

"Bald is best," Klaus insisted. "Big power. Like bone!"

Stetler offered a fist bump. "You is beauty like Mummy," Klaus assured him. Stetler's entire head blushed.

"What about me?" Kayla asked. Her voice had a funny ring to it, almost teasing. I spun around, half-expecting another bald head.

No. Kayla's hair was long and wavy and red as a beet. I blinked for ten seconds straight. It was her old hair color. Her *real* one.

We looked like twins again.

"What'll your parents say?" I asked her.

Kayla shrugged. "Maybe I'll tell them the truth." She bounced away with a grin on her face.

She was back.

FINALLY, IT WAS TIME to say our goodbyes.

"You aren't coming back to school?" we asked Klaus.

"BLECH!" He shrank in disgust. "Having friends is more simple. No classing!"

"We'll come and visit you," I promised.

"Yeah, we will," said Darius. "I'll bring my movie scripts!"

"I call kung fu guy!" Stetler let out a roar, smashing two Creeps at once with a tiger-tail kick.

Kayla shook her head, grinning.

Not Klaus. He cleared his throat roughly. "Friends is no UNDERSTANDING," he said, exasperated. "Friends is good. Friends seeing great holy city of bones...meeting Mummy and Daddy...becoming perfect true friends!"

"Yeah," we said awkwardly. "Sure."

"This is BEST," Klaus agreed. "Because perfect true friends no have breathe. No alive." He paused. "Perfect true friends...ONLY BONES!"

There was a sound like a skyscraper rising out of the earth. I spun around.

The *Creeposaurus rex* stood above me. Its massive, fanged jaw opened wide. I could not even scream.

CHOMP!

I died.

49

THE END.

Did you like my fantastic true story? No? You don't think I died? Okay, fine. I was making things up. But in my defense, what actually happened was fifty times weirder.

I felt a huge pressure squeezing my body. My bones squished, then dissolved, and I slid through the Creeposaurus's teeth like red jelly.

The next thing I heard was a scream.

"I GOT IT! I GOT HIS BONELESS BODY ON FILM!"

Darius raised his phone in the air like a Golden Globe Award. Kayla and Stetler looked shocked.

Klaus was laughing hysterically. "Funny joking, HAHA! Only joke!" He slapped my spine once it fully reformed. "Is like I explaining! BIG POWER!"

I swayed on my feet, feeling numb. Apparently there was a lot I still didn't know about my new body...

Nevertheless, it turned out there was one thing Klaus DID want before we went back.

"Group picture! For special collecting!"

Darius propped his phone against a coffin, set the timer, then scurried into position as we stood arm-in-arm around Klaus's corkboard.

SNAP! SNAP! SNAP!

The phone flashed again and again. We must've struck dozens of poses. Silly ones. Laughing ones. After the first few, we started passing the cowboy hat around. It was pretty hilarious. All the wrinkles and slime made the hat look surprisingly real.

To me, at least.

Anyway, we were all laughing so hard, we barely noticed the woman crossing into the Tomb. Her huge belly heaved with emotion (and maybe some kind of stomach bug) as she cried out, "FEE! FI! FO! FUM!"

Sorry, wrong line.

"FOUND! YOU! AT! LAST!"

It was Mrs. Fawcett, our chaperone. Her eyes glittered menacingly. She was angry and out of breath, climbing over the bone that kept the Tomb from re-sealing. Her stomach gurgled so loud, it had ECHOES.

"A-Are you all right, Mrs. Fawcett?" we asked.

"I AM FINE!" she shrieked. "UNLIKE YOU!"

Chest heaving, she pulled a long object out of her waistband.

"Miscreants! Insufferable brats! How dare you try to run from your captor? How dare you!"

"Our captor?"

"No, Mrs. Fawcett, we weren't——"

"SILENCE! Your excuses may work on Ms. Wellington, but I am not so naïve. I know the truth in your hearts!"

WHOOSH! She swung her arm. The object in her hand quickly tripled in size.

"A yardstick," I gasped. "A portable yardstick!"

Mrs. Fawcett brandished it like a whip. "Not so funny now, is it? I'll have you know, Principal Chillbody has granted me broad disciplinary powers. He does not tolerate open revolt. Nor do I!"

She stomped forward, then instantly doubled up, wincing. Loud gurgles rose from her stomach. When she recovered she looked, if possible, even madder.

"WHERE ARE THE RESTROOMS?" she roared. "FILTHY BRATS! TELL ME WHERE YOU HAVE HIDDEN THEM!"

"She's gone insane," Stetler whispered.

Mrs. Fawcett raised the yardstick again. Eyes glinting, and with her other hand clutching her stomach, she ran at us. "AAAAAARRRRGGGGHHHH!" she shrieked.

"Waaaahhhhhh!" shouted everyone. And then—

RAAAAWWWWRRRR!!!

The *Creeposaurus rex* reared up behind us. Its mighty skull glowed as red as a siren as it let loose a heart-stopping roar.

Yes. I'd flung out my power. At the same time, I felt Klaus do it, too. Together, we brought the *Creeposaurus rex* to the foreground.

Mrs. Fawcett screamed in terror. She lurched from side to side, desperate to stop herself. Her heels skidded. She clutched her belly in fright.

For a split-second, I saw it squirming inside of her clothes. It shook like a bowling ball.

"Unnngh...Arrghh...Nnnoooo..."

There was a horrible trumpeting noise; then a SPLAT!

Mrs. Fawcett stared at her feet. So did we.

So did the dang Creeposaurus!

A second later, the most vile smell in the universe spread through our nostrils. I sniffed once and almost threw up.

"We should go," I gasped.

"Y-Y-Yes!"

"Right away!"

Thumbs in our noses, we turned to Klaus. "Uh...bye!" we said. "Enjoy...staying!"

But even Klaus seemed to hesitate. His eyes flushed as he desperately plugged up his nostrils. "Smelling so bad...there is taste!" he exclaimed. And despite his pledge to remain in the Tomb from now on, he ran out.

Go online if you don't believe me.

We've got the whole thing on film.

EPILOGUE

Excerpts from *The Triosset Tribune.*

STUDENT FILM 'TAKES' THE PRIZE!

Twelve-year-old wunderkind Darius 'Leg-Sweeper' Moreland dishes on his shocking Grand Prix award, his love of Spielberg, and making films with effects that rival big budget studios. Also inside: an interview with leads Kayla Caine and Arlo Vreeland, plus karate tips from The Bone Taker's breakout star, Craig Stetler. [See BONE, A3]

CRITICS: NEW EXHIBIT IS "DINO-MITE!"

Look out, Triosset! The Vreelands are coming! The famously quarrelsome brothers are poised to unveil a new, joint exhibit featuring dozens of newly discovered (and shockingly complete) dinosaur skeletons. [See BROS, B8]

IS DR. FOSSIL CRACKING UP?

Strange clicking sounds? Bones rising to life after dark? It sounds like the plot to his twelve-year-old son's latest movie. But according to recent 911 transcripts obtained by this newspaper, Dr. Harold Vreeland seems to believe the fossils he brings home from work have been roaming his house late at night... [See YES, C2]

ALSO BY SCOTT CHARLES

Read the rest of the Creeptown series!

THE FINAL INGREDIENT
THE BONE TAKER
THE BREAKING GAME (SUMMER 2021)
TECH SUPPORT (A CREEPTOWN SHORT STORY)

Or check out my other books! (Okay. One book.)

MYLO AND MAX BREAK THE WORLD

What? You've already read them? No? You're too AFRAID to read more? Look, I get it. No judgment! But in that case, you should *definitely* find me online at www.Scott-Charles.com and add your name to …

THE SCOTT CHARLES NEWSLETTER!

Get the knowledge you need to stay far, far away from future Creeptown releases, as well as other thrilling, no-nonsense books about tough situations, such as Pixie infestation and piano recitals gone wrong, which are, quote, *"just too intense for my William. No thank you!"*

ABOUT THE AUTHOR

SCOTT CHARLES is the author of *Creeptown*, a horror adventure series for young readers, and the standalone adventure *Mylo and Max Break the World*. He writes thrilling books for busy kids who might not want to be reading, but what choice do they have? Zero! None!

Scott grew up in a pair of small towns outside of Princeton, New Jersey. He attended Duke University, where he graduated with a B.A. in Public Policy and successfully summoned [REDACTED]. He enjoys the spoils of his dastardly deal at his home in Charlotte, North Carolina. You can find him at the library, across a chess board, or on a soccer field late, late at night.

Made in the USA
Middletown, DE
03 September 2021